'I do have scruples,' I say.
'Show me.' Mrs Brown [illegible] here my
legs join u[illegible]iden.
'Uuhm,' [illegible]
'Look,' I s[illegible]osition.'
'Not yet I'[illegible] with a
few straigh[illegible]ficult
ones later.'
'This is ver[illegible] floorwards.
'I'm suppos[illegible] something on you.'
'What a good idea,' purrs my client's wife. 'Why don't you
start with your body?'



To Robin Askwith and Anthony Booth
with affection and gratitude

## Also by Timothy Lea

CONFESSIONS OF A POP PERFORMER
CONFESSIONS FROM A HEALTH FARM
CONFESSIONS FROM THE SHOP FLOOR
CONFESSIONS OF A LONG-DISTANCE LORRY DRIVER
CONFESSIONS OF A PLUMBER'S MATE

Timothy Lea

# Confessions of a Private Dick

Futura Publications Limited

A Futura Book

First published in Great Britain in 1975
by Futura Publications Limited



ISBN 0 8600 7262 2

Printed in Great Britain by
Hazell Watson & Viney Ltd
Aylesbury, Bucks

Futura Publications Limited
Warner Road, London S.E.5

## CONTENTS

# CHAPTER ONE

In which Timmy and brother-in-law, Sid, find themselves out of a job and Sid has a brainwave.

'I still don't understand how she knew that he knew,' says Sid. 'When he went down to the waterfront in the rain and they fished the two stiffs out of the drink, the D.A. gave him a funny sort of smile. Did that mean that he knew as well?'

'Search me, Sid,' I say. 'I lost touch when the bloke in the wheelchair opened up with his artificial leg. That bird had a nice pair, didn't she?'

I see immediately that my observation has given offence. ' "That bird had a nice pair"! ' snorts Sid. 'Is that all you can think about? I'm trying to have an intelligent conversation about the plot of the film and all you can do is give vent to your knocker complex. Can't you raise your mind to anything higher?'

'There wasn't much higher than those bristols,' I say. 'Honestly, Sid, that girl had curves in places where other people don't have places.'

'I still can't understand it,' muses Sid. 'Maybe they cut something out of it. All those bleeding commercials. They have to make room for them somehow.'

'They make it so difficult to follow, don't they?' I say. 'I was wondering who that mysterious bird was who kept running down the beach every half hour. I never cocoed it was a cigar commercial.'

'You only watch when there's a bird on the screen, don't

you?' says Sid. 'The television companies are wasting their time putting out programmes with blokes as far as you're concerned. I'd have thought you'd have had enough after our trip home with Nancy and Felicity.'

Do those names ring a bell? If the answer is yes you may well have come across them in *Confessions of a Plumber's Mate*. I certainly did. What a right couple of nautical ravers they were. Employed to look decorative on the poop deck of the SK498 at the Indoor Outdoor Exhibition but, in reality, knocking back a couple of bottles of 'Southern Courage – the drink that lost the South the American Civil War' – and taking it out on Sid and myself – not so much taking it out as ripping it out! Small wonder that we lost control of the boat as well as ourselves and drove off the marina and through the exit doors at Earls Court. That was all right because the boat was designed to travel on land as well as water. The only drawback was that it did not travel so well under water. We found that out when we ran up the back of a car transporter on the Chelsea Embankment and dived into the Thames. Frankly, I thought we had less chance of coming up than a winning line on a pools coupon but we surfaced just opposite Battersea Funfair – or where it used to be. A bloke who was about to commit suicide by jumping off Battersea Bridge took one look at us and fell backwards in a dead faint – actually, I must be honest, I made that last bit up. Sorry, Mum always said I was a whimsical child.

By the time we get ashore, the romance is deader than a set of election promises and we have drunk all the Southern Courage – or maybe the two things are connected. The girls get a taxi out of our lives and we get a 49 bus leaving a trail of bubbles behind us where the SK498 gets its head down for a long kip on the bed of the Thames.

'I hope that the whole distressing incident is not shambolic of the future of British industry,' says Sid as we sip our tea and watch the little pinpoint of light die away in the middle of the telly screen.

'Symbolic,' I say, thinking as I speak that Sid may be right. 'Crispin isn't exactly going to cream his jeans over this lot, is he?'

'I've been thinking about Crispin,' says Sid.

Just in case your shop was sold out, or in a fit of reckless madness, you thought you could exist without *Confessions of a Plumber's Mate* – or you have forgotten – let me point out that Crispin Fletcher is our interior decorator boss/partner who has been instrumental in securing us the job of maintenance men at the Indoor Outdoor Exhibition. As I have intimated, first indications suggest that he is going to be less than totally satisfied with our latest contribution to the profit/loss account of Home Enhancers.

'What have you been thinking?' I say.

'I've been thinking that I might have made a mistake,' says Sid.

This statement affects me like an Irish navvy stamping out his cigar butt on my groin. Though speedy to confess to weakness in others, Sid has never won renown for pointing the rigid digit in his own direction.

'Mistake, Sid?' I say.

'Well,' Sid double banks his lips in a north-easterly direction and waggles his mits. 'More an error of judgement than a mistake. A miscalculation.' I breathe more easily. For a moment I thought that Sid's subterranean passage had played havoc with his down the drains. 'There is a stage beyond Crispin.'

This is indeed interesting news. I had always thought that Crispin went about as far as you could go. It is not everybody that wears pink velvet kneebreeches and sabots – especially when they are pushing a wire basket round the supermarket. I know because I saw him. He was wheeling fourteen avocados and a jar of vaseline at the time – don't ask me, your guess is as good as mine.

'When I decided to turn my back on big business,' says Sid who was sacked from his position at the Slumbernog Bedding Company – 'And decided that there was too much capital investment involved in the transport business' – two-thirds of the Nogget transport fleet was wiped out by unfortunate accidents involving ladies – 'I was approaching the answer: fewer hands make light broth and keep the overheads down.'

'I see,' I say, wondering what he is rabbiting on about.

'Home Enhancers was right in concept but it was a mistake to get involved with Crispin. Even one other bloke can be one bloke too many. There are misunderstandings, personality clashes. What you need is a really lightweight operation: one bloke issuing the orders and another bloke carrying them out with scrupulous attention to detail.'

'I see,' I say. 'So you're not going to give Crispin another chance?'

If Sid perceives that there is a trace of sarcasm in my voice he is a master at disguising it. 'I don't think so,' he says. 'I don't think there would be any point.' At that moment, the telephone rings. Sid puts down his cuppa and strolls across the lounge of his sumptuous Vauxhall pad. 'Hello, Crispin,' he says as the earpiece nestles against his earhole. That is all he does say. He listens for a while and then stares into the mouthpiece like he reckons Crispin might be just visible through the little holes.

'What did he say?' I ask.

Sid puts the phone down. 'He agrees with me.'

'Well, that's that then,' I say. 'Back to the Labour. It's

getting so crowded these days you have to be early to be sure of a chair.'

'I know,' says Sid. 'It's hard work, isn't it? They ought to send it to you through the post. Think of all the clerical staff it would save. One bloke could probably do the whole thing.'

'Yes, but that would make the others redundant,' I explain. 'Then they'd all go on strike, wouldn't they?'

'If they were redundant, it wouldn't matter, would it?' says Sid. 'They couldn't do anything.'

'They'd probably picket the place so the one bloke who was doing all the work couldn't get in,' I say.

Sid's face contorts in anger. 'Bastards!' he says. 'No wonder this country's going to the dogs when bloody bolsheviks can prevent you getting your unemployment benefit. What's the ordinary working man expected to do?'

Further discussion on this interesting point is interrupted by the arrival of a taxi outside the front door. Out of it gets my sister and Sid's wife – only one person as regular readers will recall – in a soaking wet condition and wearing an expression that would be rejected by a voodoo mask maker as being likely to frighten off prospective customers. Since we are both well acquainted with her vindictive nature and could be accused of having contributed to her bedraggled condition (she fell in the marina when the SK498 went beserk) it is a matter of seconds before we are letting ourselves out by the back door.

'A taxi,' says Sid. 'That's marvellous, isn't it? Even if I had a million quid I could never travel in a taxi. I'd feel awkward somehow. But it doesn't worry her, does it?'

'I expect she's more adaptable,' I say diplomatically. I could also say that, thanks to the success of the boutiques and the wine bars, Rosie is a blooming sight nearer to a million quid than her old man and therefore able to afford the odd taxi, but I deem it inadvisable. There is no doubt that Sid's half-baked schemes to make money at any cost are a direct result of Rosie's successful moola-making activities.

'Hello, Dad Dad.' The appealing waif fondling his ferret through the bars of its cage with a length of bamboo cane is my nephew, Jason Noggett – or 'The Child Pirhana' as he is known in some circles.

'Don't poke him like that,' says Sid. 'He doesn't like it.'

'When you buy Jason rabbit, Dad Dad?' says the little fiend looking up towards the house thoughtfully.

Sid opens the back gate. 'I've told you! You're not having one until we get another cage.'

'That's right,' I say. 'We don't want Mr Ferret to gobble bunny up, do we?'

Jason flashes me a quick 'Piss off, Uncle Timmy!' look and continues to address his father. 'Mummy home now? Daddy go boozer?'

'I'm having a word with your uncle,' says Sid irritably. 'Where's Jerome?'

'We play Red Indians,' says Jason, giving his ferret a last affectionate poke. 'He staked out on ant hill.'

In fact, it is only the manure heap next door but the child is in a very anti-social condition.

'I don't know what's got into that child,' says Sid when we have handed over some 'sweety money' blackmail and been allowed to continue on our way. 'He's never wanted for anything – except that alligator he's always on about – and yet he's a real handful.'

'Kids today,' I say in my best 'old codgers' manner.

'That's right,' says Sid. 'Sometimes I think we're cruel when we try to be kind. You give them too much and they miss out on the simple things.'

'Still, it's a violent age, isn't it?' I say. 'That's got to have an effect on them.'

'Must have an effect on all of us,' says Sid. 'Still, it's always been like that, hasn't it? Look at that film on the telly this afternoon. Every time that bloke stuck the brim of his fedora round the frosted glass somebody bashed him over the nut.'

'And it wasn't just "The Mob" was it?' I say. 'Those Bay City cops were really mean, weren't they? You needed a paper bag to put your teeth in if you went round to report that your cat was missing.'

'Yet all the time he preserved a kind of simple dignity, didn't he?' says Sid admiringly. 'One man against a corrupt society – and pulling all the crumpet on the side. Can't be bad.' He suddenly clutches my arm. 'Timmo! I've just had an idea.' Strong men – and ones with brains – run when Sid says that but I stand my ground bravely. 'You know he worked out of that office above the launderette?'

'You need capital to set up a launderette,' I say. 'Anyway, all the best sites have gone.'

'I didn't mean that!' says Sid. 'I was referring to the simplicity of the operation. All you need is a telephone. You could do it from home.'

'Mum wouldn't stand for it,' I say. 'All that washing everywhere. Where would you hang it?'

'Forget about the bloody washing!' shouts Sid so loud that an old lady wheels her shopping basket into a lamp post. 'I'm talking about becoming a private detective. Don't you see? It's perfect. No overheads, no partners, no qualifications. Crime is the only growth industry in this country at the moment and more people are getting divorced than get married. We can't go wrong. What's more, it's legit.'

'Yeah,' I breathe, buying my imagination a one-way ticket to romantic places. 'I can just see it: "Timothy Lea, Private Dick".'

## CHAPTER TWO

In which Timmy is shown round office accommodation by Teresa, a shapely coloured lady with whom he strikes up an immediate understanding.

'I find it very unsavoury,' says Mum.

'So do I,' says Dad pushing his plate away. 'I think it was a mistake to fry it. I never heard of anybody frying spaghetti.'

'I thought it would make a change,' says Mum. 'It seems wicked to throw food away these days. Anyway, I wasn't talking about that. I was referring to this detective business. I don't like to think of Timmy getting mixed up with a lot of criminals.'

'You've left it a bit late to express concern in that direction, haven't you?' sneers Dad. 'It's the criminals you ought to start feeling sorry for. Get your precious Sidney amongst them and they'll be asking for police protection. He'll be in his element with a load of Bernards.' (Bernard Dillon: Villain. Ed.)

'Do you want your father's spaghetti?' sniffs Mum. 'There's some more gravy.'

I decline gracefully and wonder how Mum manages to get that distinctive roasted flavour into the tea.

'I hope the neighbours don't get to hear about it,' says Dad. 'You remember what it was like when Mrs Brown's boy became a copper. Nobody would speak to the family for three months. Even when he got busted for nicking the Doctor Barnardo's box, people were slow to forgive. It won't be easy for your mother and I if the news gets out. We're well thought of in this neighbourhood.'

'Only because people think you're a fence,' I say. 'All that stuff you nick from work. It's no wonder we had that bloke round with the rings.'

Dad's habit of knocking off items from the lost-property office where he works has not gone unnoticed by the neighbours. Probably because he has an unhealthy leaning towards large stuffed animals that do not fit snugly into any of the suitcases he has nicked. Talking of suitcases, I remember how when I was a kid I used to think he was a conjurer. He brought home this blooming enormous suitcase, opened it, took out another suitcase, opened it, took out another suitcase, opened it, took out— in the end he had six suitcases and a set of cork table mats with the pattern nearly faded away. I remember how disappointed I was with the table mats because they did not do anything. It was like a game of pass-the-parcel when you end up with a tooth brush.

'I've never done anything to reproach myself with,' moans Dad. 'I've served three kings and a queen and none of them found cause to point the finger at me. They weren't half-inched, those rings. They'd just fallen off the back of a lorry, that's all.'

'Must have been why most of the stones had jumped out of their settings,' I say. 'You were done there, there's no doubt about it.'

'The boy's right, Walter,' says Mum. 'That eternity ring you gave me dissolved the first time I did the washing up.'

Dad is still shouting about ingratitude as I go out of the door. Sid has made me responsible for finding us an office and I have an appointment with a Miss Bradford who is going to show me some offices at 'my end of the market'. I remember the phrase because the geezer I spoke to on the phone underlined it when I told him how much we were willing to pay. Sid has a theory that it is an advantage for a private eye to have an office on the shady side of town and there seems little likelihood of him failing to achieve his aim.

Miss Bradford is richly knockered and has a dark complexion – very dark. In fact she is black all over, or, at least, all the parts I can see. Hold my bike for a minute and I'll check. I gaze with interest at the way the waft and weft of her sweater is being stretched asunder by the thrust of her bust and then move up to her wide brown eyes. Two of them, placed on either side of her hooter to achieve maximum effect. She seems surprised to see me.

'You're much younger than the fellers I usually show round,' she says. 'What are you, a designer, commercial artist?'

'I'm a dick,' I say. The moment I hear how it sounds I wish I hadn't. 'A private investigator,' I correct myself.

Miss Bradford nods. 'Good, I thought you might need a lot of daylight for your work. In most of the places I'll be showing you, you wouldn't be able to see if you were holding your pencil the right way round unless the light was on.'

'Where are you from?' I say, always dynamite when it comes to casual banter.

'Peckham,' she says.

'I meant before that.'

'Southwark.' Her eyes send tracer bullets towards mine. 'You thought I was going to say Bongo Bongo, didn't you?'

'South Bongo Bongo,' I say. 'I'm from Clapham, myself. Europe's Disneyland. It's looking lovely this time of year. The goal mouths are cutting up a bit but you can't have everything, can you?'

Miss Bradford does not reply to my question and I sense that the state of the football pitches in my homeland is not of prime concern to her. There is more than a touch of the

Matilda Ngoblas about her and it is a real trip down mammary lane to case those bounteous boobs. Matilda, faithful readers will recall, used to be one of our next door neighbours at 17 Scraggs Lane, ancestral home of the Leas since times immoral and it was with her that I proved that two young people can reach across the barriers of race and colour, and have it off on the sitting-room carpet just like you and me – well, just like me and your sister. Unfortunately, Dad's unexpected arrival put the kibosh on that spot of instant romance but I see no reason why lightning Lea should not strike twice.

'What do you think of it?'

I wrench my mince pies off Miss Bradford's bristols and look round the room. 'This is where the bluebottles come to die, is it?' I say with a light laugh.

'It needs cleaning up,' agrees the comely blackamoor. 'Still, what do you expect for the money you're prepared to pay? It's a wonder you're not working out of a telephone box.'

We would have been if Sid had thought of it, I muse to myself idly tracing 'fuck' in the dust on top of the desk – well, it makes a change from 'clean me', doesn't it? One thing I do like about the office is the frosted glass in the door that gives out on to the corridor. Just right for grabbing a trailer of Lauren Bacall's profile or the outline of the two hoods who have come to bounce you off the walls. I can just see myself behind the desk reaching out for the two fingers of Tizer that live in the top right hand drawer and – hang on a minute! The profile outside the door is not at all the kind of thing I was thinking of. It is of some geezer armed with an enormous hard going into orbit at an angle of forty-five degrees to his body. I glance at Miss Bradford and see that she has clocked this new threat to our already over-congested airways. An expression more of interest than of outrage hovers around her dusky chops. This is too much! I always suspected that flashers had big ones and this proves it. Filthy brute, going around making everyone discontented with their lot – or in my case, not such a lot.

'Excuse me,' I say briskly. 'I must put an end to this.'

'Just what I was thinking,' murmurs Miss Bradford wistfully.

I try not to think what she means by that remark and wrench open the door. Maybe if I gave the bloke 10p he would go and stand outside somebody else's office.

'Now look— !' I begin. I stop when I see an old man holding a broom at his side. 'All right?' I say weakly.

The old man looks me up and down as if he finds it a very unrewarding occupation. 'Your flies are undone,' he says. I mumble something and close the door.

Miss Bradford is laughing. 'I thought that was too good to be true,' she says.

'Yeah. Looked er – a bit funny, didn't it?' I say.

'Looked like the answer to a maiden's prayer,' says Miss Bradford. 'That's what sent you bustling to the door, wasn't it? You didn't like the competition.'

'I don't think of flashers as competition,' I say. 'They do that instead of the real thing.' I turn my back and do up my fly.

'Are you going to give me a demonstration?' mocks Miss B.

'What of?' I say.

'That's up to you. You're handling the equipment.'

'I'm not handling it,' I say. 'I'm readjusting my clothing.'

'Are you shy?' she says.

If I was going to be honest, I would say yes. Self-confident birds always knock me back on my heels and this one is a spade to boot. We all know what they're like, don't we? Carrying a black anaconda between their legs and blessed with a natural sense of rhythm. It is not the dancing I am worrying about as much as the ballroom if you take my meaning. Percy is no pouch slouch but size-wise he may fall a few feet short of what Miss Bradford is used to when the tom toms beat out their jungle love call to the tum tums.

'Shy?' I say with the suspicion of an amazed laugh. 'Me? Ouch!' I have just stumbled back against the filing cabinet and those handles do stick in your back, don't they? The whole structure gives a hollow rumble and I clear my throat uneasily. 'This comes with it, does it?'

Miss Bradford gazes into my minces as if she expects the answer to my question to come up on them like a telex machine. 'It's funny about white skin,' she says as if talking to herself. 'It looks so soft.' She reaches up and draws her hand down the side of my cheek. 'Terry likes it.'

'Does he?' I say. 'What a pity he's not here. I could have—'

'She is here,' says Miss Bradford propping her bristols against my all the best. 'I'm Terry. Short for Teresa.'

'It's funny you should say that,' I say. 'I've always been partial to – er br-bl-col—'

'Black pussy,' says Terry helpfully. 'I could tell by the way you were looking at me that you wanted to get my panties off.'

'Ye-es,' I say. Terry Bradford is what you might call direct when it comes to filling in the plot.

'But you're not going to get the chance.' My spirits fall and percy suspends his clumsy clamber into the vertical. Could it be that I am in the presence of a prick teaser – or prick Teresa as seems more nearly the case? 'I'm not wearing any.'

This is interesting news and delivered in terms that invite verification – good word that, isn't it? I think I will be using it a lot when I become a private dick: 'I'm going to have to ask you to verify that alibi, Mrs Cholmondeley.' Terry's well-defined lips are hovering before the identical feature on my own Jem Mace and a tilt of the nut is all it requires to set the merry scamps clambering over each other. Whilst the bits that stop your cakeholes from fraying are thus pleasurably engaged, I slip one of my germans up the back of Terry's dress and feel the overhang of her well-defined sit feature cutting into her thighs. Some birds have back bumpers like a couple of under-filled water cushions but this chick is the last load out of the melon field. Firm as a weightlifter's handshake and definitely unhampered by any contact with the knicker counter of Marks and Sparks. It is probably my imagination set off by her own comments on white flesh but there seems to be a tougher texture to her skin. More tensility. It all helps build up the impression of strength and formidableness that is restraining the progress of my hampton towards the ceiling. Will the midnight mauler of the Clapham Common children's playground sand pit be a match for the coloured snatch? That is the question the free world is asking itself at this time. Normally my action man kit would be pointing towards the airholes in my hooter but at the moment it is a quarter to nine and losing time fast. A most unusual occasion when you consider the proximity of this obviously willing curve carnival. Wake up Lea! What has got into the marrow arrow that it seems unlikely to get into anything else? Most of the time my mind and body work independently. Now, my fears of being found wanting threatens to prevent me from slipping my fun gunny into this jungle bunny.

Terry pulls back her head and brushes her lips to and

fro across mine. At hip level her crutch imitates the motion and I feel like a piece of carved wood that is being polished. My right hand hovers around the slit in the collecting box and I probe the soft, tight curls; feeling the whole feature quiver beneath my fingertips. As I had imagined they might, Terry's hands drop to my waist and she fumbles untidily with the catch of my trousers. Just when I am thinking that she may need help, the zip jerks downwards and my slack cock is exposed like a fish in a net dangling against the side of a vessel. Terry sucks in her breath and dips a mit down the front of my Y-fronts.

'Oooom!' she says. 'That's nice.'

I don't think she is tempted to write to the Guinness Book of Records about it but the remark is just what percy needs to get all pinky and perky. Make no mistake about it, ladies. You can work wonders with a shy, sensitive lad if you give him a bit of admiration and encouragement. 'What an attractive spot to have a prick' or 'Goodness! I doubt if my slight frame will be able to withstand the onslaught of such a monster', go down a lot better than 'Everything seems to be miniaturised these days, doesn't it?' or 'OK, vole parts, let's be having you!'

The minute that percy hears Teresa's comforting words he responds as if plugged into a recharging machine. Any hint of the horizontal is brushed aside by a new sense of dynamic purpose and an angel choir bursts into song. Actually, it is somebody turning on a transistor radio across the other side of the light well but it does make me think about where we are. Miss Bradford has now started to fondle my spheroids and it is clear that a desire for intimacy is somewhat nearer than the back of her mind.

'Nice black pussy,' she husks bullying my lower lip with both of hers. My right hand has now discovered an opening with great opportunities for advancement and I look around for somewhere to start thrusting my way to the top. Though not expecting a four poster bed to be lowered through the ceiling on silken ropes it would be nice if there was somewhere a little more prepossessing than rutted, crumbling lino to plight our troth on. You could blight it rather than plight it in these surroundings. Still, it is no good worrying too much. We are lucky to have the desire, the opportunity and the capability. A stand-up quickie against the side of the filing cabinet seems to be the order of the day. Be just like the office party, won't it? You always fancied that shy girl in accounts but you never knew she was like that – not until you poured half a bottle of gin into her lemonade.

In practice, the filing cabinet rattles too much so we stagger back against the door that connects with the next office. Teresa has thoughtfully yanked my trousers and pants down to knee level and percy is peering through the curtain of my shirt like an actor looking to see if the theatre is filling up. It would be but a second's work to engage the lady's parts with my towing equipment but I feel that those lovely knockers deserve closer inspection. As I have already indicated, Teresa is handing out a terrible beating to the front of her sweater and I almost hear the fibres groan with relief as I start to put the merchandise on display. What a hammockful! She may not wear any knicks but she needs a bra in case she turns round quickly and kills someone. Talk about Black Beauties. She makes Chesty Morgan seem like Olive Oil's kid sister on a diet. Some birds stuff a handkerchief between their knockers. This chick could manage a couple of sheets – and you wouldn't have to take them off the bed first. Of course, I exaggerate a trifle – I exaggerate a jelly if you give me half a chance – but this bird is definitely an experience bristol-wise. For a moment I gawp. Then my itching fingers flip up the bra cups like they are garage doors. Bouncing out to meet me come a couple of nipples like the last third of a brown cucumber. She is obviously pleased with them because her hands leave my hampton and thrust up her bristols until the nipples are tickling my bracket.

'You like black titties?' she says. I don't answer her because I have my mouth full. Miss Bradford would clearly prefer it if I had two cakeholes or one very wide one because she keeps counter punching with her knockers until I am in danger of going down for the count – as opposed to the cunt which is what I normally go down for. This is all very, very well but my appetite is now sufficiently worked up for the main course – shish kebab of Teresa Bradford: tender portions of grumble and grunt speared on my steaming hampton and cooked over a couple of white hot balls. I am about to pocket the lady's socket on my sprocket when she gives a shudder like a cabinet minister looking at the latest trade figures and dives down the front of my body until her Manchesters are pummelling my knee caps. What those soft, tender lips and talented tongue are dishing out I hesitate to reveal but it is not a million miles from what must go on in the testing department of a trumpet factory. I am not surprised that the Queen is looking the other way as she salutes – she is on a calendar on the far wall of the office.

Teresa slips a hand between my legs and – OOOOOOOOOOOOHHHHH!!' Any more of that and I will be using her epiglotis as the spring-up target for my fun gun. Taking a deep breath and hoping that Teresa will not do the same, I haul the sensational syrup (syrup of figs: nigs Ed.) up my power-packed frame and cup my hands under her back bumpers. As our lips collide I hitch her into the air and guide her into the right position for a quick game of furry quoits. Her helpful fingers pull back percy from his streamlined – or more like it, steamlined – position against my body and I slowly ease her down until her feet are resting on top of mine and percy is flying blind. She grinds slowly whilst my nervous system responds like an under cranked pin table with two balls running and everything lighting up at the same time.

'Love that white flesh!' she groans, stretching her long fingers down the back of my thighs and chewing my neck. Call me impulsive if you like – though I usually answer to Tiger Lips – but all the signs indicate that this is going to be a quick romance. Miss Bradford presses her body against mine at many points and I lift her into the air so that her knees are on either side of my thighs and proceed to see how far percy can push pussy without losing contact. Teresa clearly likes this game and it is not long before her knees are banging against the connecting door like a couple of battering rams. My eyes glaze over and it seems as if the Queen is sliding off her horse – I know how she feels.

'Go on! Go on!' I never know why women say things like that because you have no intention of stopping, do you? I press back against the door for the last, telling thrusts and – 'AAAAAAAAARRRRGGGG!!!' No, you're wrong. That's not me going into orbit. Some blooming idiot has opened the door. Still carrying Teresa with me, I take a series of increasingly fast backwards steps and collapse on what turns out to be a button-back sofa. We must look as if we are doing a speeded up tango. My crutch needs one – or a couple of splints – and my high-pitched yelp of pain threatens to shatter the lamp bowl. When I have moved Teresa to a part of my body that is not a disaster area, I look over her shoulder and see a middle-aged bag of coke looking over his specs at us and rubbing his hands together nervously.

'Righty ho,' he says. 'Glad you could make it.'

He goes behind a desk – I mean, of course, that he takes a seat behind a desk – and I try and work out what makes him so certain that we have made it. I am not so sure myself and I should be one of the first to know. At least he is being very reasonable about the whole thing. A lot of people would react very badly if you charged into their office in full knee tremble. Teresa pulls down the shutters over her knockers and I sweep the remains of percy into my Y-fronts. I will have to hold the autopsy later. The geezer in the blue pin stripe leans forward on his desk and places his fingertips together.

'Of course, that's all very gratifying,' he muses, waving a hand in the direction of his left earhole. 'But how are we to know it's not just a flash in the pan? It's when you're waiting in the anteroom that you really get to grips with it, isn't it? You realize what you're letting yourself in for.'

This bloke is leaving me behind fast. If he is handing out a mild bollocking, I don't get it. And why is he smiling at us like that? He reminds me of the bloke who came up to me when I was having a gypsy's kiss in the gents at Piccadilly Underground – not a pursuit I recommend, incidentally.

'We'd better be going,' says Teresa.

'But you've only just come,' says Pin Stripe. There he goes! Jumping to conclusions again. 'I know it's awkward talking to a complete stranger about intimate matters but don't worry, we've all been through it.' He smiles at Teresa when he says this and I wonder if he means what I think he means. She was certainly very friendly when you come to think about it. The bloke unscrews a fountain pen and pulls a pad towards him. 'How long have you two been together?'

'Since about ten o'clock this morning,' I say.

The smile drops faster than a pair of lead knickers. 'Ten o'clock this morning and you're here already?'

'It wasn't very far, was it?' I say, turning to Teresa. 'We wasted a bit of time trying to park but—'

'You can't expect things to work out right from the beginning,' says the bloke. 'There's got to be a period of acclimatization. You know what that means, don't you?'

'Oh yes,' I say. 'It's what you have to do before you get out of a diver's suit.'

Pin Stripe does not seem to hear my remark and helps himself to a couple of pills from the pocket of his waistcoat. 'God knows, we live in troubled times and the whole fabric of society as we understand it is threatened – but really! You have to give it a little more time than this! What makes you think you have problems when you've only been married four hours – Good God!' He strikes his forehead with his clenched fist. 'You made the appointment yesterday – before you were even married!'

Before we can say anything, the door behind us has burst open and a bloke with a black eye and scratch marks down his cheek is revealed dragging a screaming woman by the hair. 'Sorry we're late, guv,' he says. 'We had words on the way here.'

While the couple trade punches in the doorway and Pin Stripe slides beneath his desk with a strangled croak, I am busy reading the sign stencilled on the office door. It says: 'J. Bugstrode, Marriage Guidance Counsellor.'

## CHAPTER THREE

In which Timmy sets out to obtain evidence in a divorce case and, after a brush with gentle Gretchen, comes up against demanding Mrs Brown.

'Not much happening, is there?' says Sid.

It is three days after my first visit to the building which now houses the N.I.B. (Noggett Investigation Bureau) and Sid and I are well and truly esconced – as El Sid chooses to call it. This means that we have straightened out all the paper clips and folded them again, and watched Mr J. Bugstrode taken away by a couple of men in white coats. I have not said anything to Sid about Mr Bugstrode and Teresa Bradford. I don't feel that it would help anybody, somehow.

Sid picks up the telephone and holds it to his ear. 'It's working,' he says.

'Don't worry, Sid,' I say. 'The word's got to get around, hasn't it? We're not in the book or anything like that. Those leaflets we dropped off in the Co-op are going to take a few days to get around. We're competing against a special offer on dried figs.'

'Funny about that bloke next door,' muses Sid. 'I wonder if there was more to it than the job. It might be blackmail, you know. He could have had a go at one of his patients.'

'Unlikely, Sid,' I say. 'These geezers are very prone to mental disorders and nervous breakdowns.'

'Exactly,' says Sid. 'He might have found that he was giving the helpful advice from inside some bloke's old lady.

The job getting on top of him in fact. Then, the door bursts open and—'

'I don't think it was like that,' I say hurriedly. 'Do you fancy a cup of cha?'

'Not from that bleeding machine, I don't,' says Sid. 'That's not powder they have at the bottom of those cups – it's rust.' He glances at his watch and picks up his new raincoat – the one which has epaulettes, panels, brass rings, restraining straps at the sleeves and is three sizes too big for him. Alan Ladd wore something like it in 'This Gun For Hire'. 'I'll leave you to look after the shop. Don't do anything stupid. Take down any messages and try to get some of that pigeon shit off the windows.'

'Where are you going?' I ask.

'I'm going round to the public library to look at the footprints.'

Before I can decide whether or not it would be wise to enquire further, Sid has gone. Opening time is not many seconds away and no doubt he has nipped off to get a bit Chopin before Lilley and Skinner. (Chopin and Liszt: pissed. Lilley and Skinner: dinner. Ed.) What can I do to while away the weary hours? I could write a few letters if I had anyone to write to, or try to unclog my biro. It has also been a long time since I pushed back the cuticles on my toenails. It hurts but at the same time you get a funny electric feeling which I quite fancy. You must know what I mean. I have not cleaned my belly button for a few months, either. My spirits rise as I see a whole programme of personal hygiene beginning to take shape. I will start on my toes and work upwards, skipping the most difficult bits until I get home.

I have just got my shoes and socks off and one of my feet on the desk when a shadow falls across the frosted glass. It does not do any damage but the shock makes me whip my tootsie off the desk and kick the telephone into the wastepaper basket. Before I can shout 'goal!', the door opens and a large, worried looking guy comes into the room. I would have preferred a beautiful blonde reeking of expensive perfume but you can't have everything.

I advance round my desk to meet him and then shuffle back as I see him looking at my bare feet.

'Hot, isn't it?' I say. 'What can I do for you, Mr – ?'

'Brown,' says the bloke. 'You handle divorce business, don't you?' His eyes follow me as I replace the receiver on the phone in the wastepaper basket.

'We're getting a new one,' I explain. 'Yes, Mr Brown. We handle divorce business. We handle anything. What's your problem?'

The man looks round and lowers his voice confidentially. 'It's my wife,' he says.

That's a relief, I think to myself. Nothing too complicated to begin with. 'Playing around, is she?' I say.

Mr Brown looks impressed. 'How did you know that? I only dropped her off at the golf club on my way here.'

I wave my hand airily. 'Just call it instinct, Mr Brown. What do you want us to do for you?'

Mr Brown buries his face in his hands. 'I can't take any more. It's too humiliating. The men – her lovers. She's insatiable.'

'In where?' I say. 'That's the Indian Ocean, isn't it? I had a mate who went there for his holidays.'

'I believe you're thinking of the Seychelles,' says the bloke. 'I was referring to my wife's sexual appetites.'

'Oh yes,' I say, keeping the professional cool that is doing so well for me. 'So your wife is in the Seychelles having it off – I mean, behaving indiscreetly, with whatever kind of person lives there, a fact that is inevitably causing you to feel dead choked?'

'My wife has never been near the Seychelles,' says the bloke beginning to turn red. 'Not that it makes much difference where she's been. She has relations everywhere.'

'We're a bit like that,' I say chattily. 'I've even got an aunty in New Zealand. Takapuna. It's north of Auckland. She sends us a Christmas card every year. Same one usually. Maybe they don't have a lot of Christmas cards down there or she bought a job lot.'

To my surprise, Mr Brown starts to quiver. 'I am not in the slightest bit interested in your aunt in New Zealand!' he hisses. 'I have other things on my mind! My wife has become an unbearable burden and I wish to rid myself of her. I want a divorce!'

'I see,' I say. 'You're sure that's really what you want? There's a bloke next door – no, he's not there any more.'

I feel sad when I think that Mr Bugstrode has taken a trip to the funny farm. We might have been able to do business together. He could have sent us the marriages he was unable to save.

'I want you to procure the evidence with which I can divorce the slut! Take photographs of her in fragrante delecto!'

'She gets abroad a lot, doesn't she?' I say. 'Prefers foreigners and that kind of thing, I suppose. A lot of birds do. Personally, I think it's all in the mind. I don't believe they're any—'

'If I could get my hands on one of those swine,' says Brown, thoughtfully gazing into space and picking up the wastepaper basket. 'I'd crumple him up like a piece of paper. I'd rip him apart!'

I watch, fascinated, as Brown folds the waste-bin in half and then tears the metal as if it is a piece of tin foil. When that look comes into his eyes I would hate to be found practising press-ups on his old lady.

'What does she look like?' I say. 'Where can I find her?'

Brown produces a much fingered photo and pushes it across the table to me. 'By the cringe!' I say 'She's a bit of—' I pause when I see how Brown is staring at me. His eyes are harder than petrified cherry stones. '– very nice, very refined.'

When you look at Brown and you look at the photograph it is not easy to relate the two. The missus is definitely a looker and a bit flash with it. Brown seems like the sort of bloke who would turn down a job as a bank clerk because he thought the uniform was too daring.

'She's booked in to the Densford Hotel,' says Brown. 'I found this card in her handbag – quite by chance, of course.'

'Of course,' I say. The card is a postcard announcing that Room Number 367 has been booked for today's date. I turn it over and see that it is addressed to a Mr Brown. 'That's not you?' I say.

'Of course it isn't!' snaps Brown. 'Don't you see? Her lover has given her that and used my name!' He starts trembling again and suddenly picks up Sid's paperknife and drives it through the desk. 'I'd go there myself but I'm frightened that I wouldn't be able to restrain myself. I only have to think of what they might be doing and—!' He brings his fist down on top of the filing cabinet and all the drawers lock. I know because I try to open one of them.

'Leave it to us,' I say soothingly and start walking towards the door in the hopes that he will follow. At this rate there will be little of the office left when Sid gets back.

'You'll take a photograph, will you?' says Brown.

'That's right,' I say, grateful for the suggestion.

Brown shakes his head. 'A dirty business. Still—' he looks me up and down – 'I suppose you're the man for it. How soon will you have results? I want this matter dealt with speedily!' He starts looking as if he is about to smash something else and I open the door like the cat has just started saying goodbye to a Richard III on a mat.

'Tomorrow evening,' I say. 'How can I get in touch with you?'

'I'll come here,' he says. 'Six o'clock?'

'Right,' I breathe.

Mr Brown's vengeful footsteps echo away down the corridor and I put my shoes and socks on. I will attack my cuticles another day. You need a bit of hot water to soften them up anyway. I could use something from the coffee machine but there is the danger that it might melt my toes off. Difficult to get your feet in the beakers, too.

I am really chuffed after my interview with Mr Brown. He seemed to accept me without question – mind you, I did handle myself well. I put him at his ease and got straight down to the nitty-gritty with the minimum of flannel. Sid will be pleased when I tell him. But why should I tell him? I have got this far by myself, why not finish the job? Close the file and tie a pink ribbon round it before throwing it on the D.A.'s desk. That's what Clint Eastwood would do. Yes, I will show Sid what a smooth operator I can be when he is not around to foul me up.

In fact, Sid is so elephants (elephant's trunk: drunk. Ed.) when he rolls back at a quarter past three that I doubt if he would understand if I did tell him. He starts reading a paperback entitled *Blondes Like It Backwards* and then falls asleep on it so that the centre spine forms a trough for his spittle. All very *Homes and Gardens*.

It occurs to me that I am going to need a flashlight camera for my assignment and that my Instamatic is not going to do, even if I run into the bedroom holding a freshly struck match above my head. Luckily I know a bag of coke who frightens American tourists into parting with a few bob by chasing them down Lower Regent Street with his camera and saying that the snaps will be waiting for them when they get back to the States – he even charges them postage. I don't think he has ever taken an actual photograph in his life but the camera looks impressive.

I wait till Sid has slouched off saying that he has got an urgent appointment and start making arrangements. My mate says that I can have the camera if I pop round for it and let him have a couple of prints if they turn out to be a bit fruity. I suppose Mr Brown is right. It is a dirty business. I would not fancy it if some geezer rushed in and started snapping away while I was exercising the pocket python. I will have to move fast in case there is unpleasantness.

One thing that worries me is when the dastardly deed is going to take place. I should have asked Mr Brown if he had an inkling but it might have set him off on a rampage. The dirty duo could be on the job at this very moment. I hope they have a lot of stamina otherwise everything might be over before I have screwed in my flash bulb. To check out this unsavoury thought I ring up the hotel and ask to speak to Mr Brown – I can always pretend to be room service if he answers – but there is no one there. Diabolically clever, isn't it? If I can keep up this form no criminal will be safe.

An hour later, I am sitting in the lounge of the Densford Hotel and wondering how I got lumbered with the disgusting thimbleful of brown liquid nestling between my thumbs. I asked for a beer and the bloke behind the bar gave me something out of a bottle with 'Byrrh' written on it. He seemed to think I was joking when I pointed out his mistake and I thought he was joking when he told me how much the muck cost. 45p! It is shocking, isn't it? Still, I suppose if you are a private eye you have to get used to ritzing it up a bit. Which reminds me, I never talked to Brown about moola. Sid was very concerned that we did not take anything on without getting some cash in advance. Not that Brown can welsh on us because he will be coming round for his photographs. We can collect then.

I take another casual gander round the room and retire behind my copy of *London Cries* – at these bar prices it should be bleeding weeping. I have checked that the key to Room 367 is in reception, now all I have to do is wait for Mrs Brown and her lover to show up. From what I saw of the photograph I would not mind being around if she was looking for something to scratch her snatch with. I hope I will be able to recognize her. Birds can change very easily. Hang on a minute! That looks like her following the two knockers into the reception area. What a figure! She makes an hour glass seem like a test tube. And that arse! It looks as if it is hovering over a warm air duct. All this and V.P.L. (visible pant line). No wonder Mr Brown gets his knickers in a twist when he thinks of other geezers giving her pussy a protein injection. I could be up that like a rat up a drain-pipe. But, restrain yourself, Lea! I must get my priorities straightened out – regular readers will not be surprised to hear that my number one priority started shaking out the kinks the moment I clapped eyes on Mrs Brown. I must keep a cool head, steady hands and a limp hampton and remember whose side I am on. To get mixed up with your clients must be fatal in this game.

The lovely Mrs Brown exchanges a smile for a room key and heads for the lift leaving a fine veil of steam rising from the desk clerk's eyeballs. When she moves away from you it is like a couple of small medicine balls nuzzling each other. I am so mesmerized that I knock back my drink without thinking. Ugh! The stuff that Dad rubs on his chest must taste better than that.

No sooner have the lift doors closed than an ugly thought assails me: I don't know what Mrs Brown's fancy man looks like. He could be anybody. I had better get up to the room and keep an eye open. There is also the question of how I am going to get into the room. The key has gone and the desk clerk is not going to give me another one. Maybe they will leave it in the door. I can see less chance of that than of it raining potatoes on St Patrick's Day. I step out of the lift, walk past the door of the room and hear what sounds like a bloke laughing and the chink of glasses. Gordon Bennett? Don't say he was in there all the time. The swine! I hope the tassel of his silk dressing-gown dangles in the ice bucket and brushes against the tip of his hampton. At any second, he may come behind her and kiss the side bit where her neck joins her shoulders. I know the kind of devilish practices these blokes get up to. Unless I move fast he will be getting in before I do. Where am I going to find a pass key or a fire escape? You don't have one on you, do you? I glance up the corridor and see a bird coming out of a room carrying an armful of bedding. Maybe she will be able to help.

'Excuse me,' I say, scampering to her side. 'You – er don't happen to have a key to three six seven, do you? I seem to – er—' I pat my chest and hope that she will reckon I have misplaced my key.

'Not your room,' she says reproachfully. Knickers! I would have to cop some central European bird with a strong sense of right and wrong.

'I am private detective,' I say. 'Like policeman. Very good.'

The bird leads the way into a small room full of laundry

baskets and shelves of sheets, and dumps the bedclothes on a pile in the corner.

'I do not know,' she says.

She is an appealing bird. Slim and with harassed wisps of hair fluffing out of her barnet. Though small she has big eyes and a wide mouth that turns up attractively at the corners.

'I only want it for a few minutes,' I say. 'I'm not going to nick anything.'

'Nick?' she says.

'Steal,' I say. 'I want to take a photograph of the inside of the room, that's all.'

The bird's face brightens. 'You can take photograph of three six five. Is same inside.'

'It's not just the room,' I say. 'It's the people as well. It's sort of – how can I explain it?'

'Surprise?' says the bird.

'That's it,' I say. 'You've got it. A surprise.' I reach out my hand hopefully.

Maybe I am going too fast because the bird does not make a move. 'It would be best thing if you ask manager, I think,' she says. Right at the back of her eyes where the dark blue is practically black, I think I can see a twinkle.

'I'm prepared to make it worth your while,' I say, feeling inside my jacket. 'I'm not asking you to do it for nothing.'

The girl stretches out a hand and pokes my forearm. It is as if she is testing a piece of meat to see if it is tender. 'Money?' she says.

'Whatever you like,' I say. Back in three six seven a naked Mrs Brown is probably swinging upside down from the chandelier while her boyfriend stands on the mantelpiece and attempts to harpoon her with his funny gun, but I sense that it would be a mistake to rush things with this particular bint. 'What's your name?' I say.

'Gretchen,' she says. 'And your name?'

'Timmy,' I say. 'Have you been over here long?'

'Six weeks,' she says.

'Made a lot of friends?'

She shakes her head sadly. 'No.'

'Oh well,' I say, giving her arm a pat. 'You've made a friend now.' I am not just saying it either. She is an appealing little bird and very fanciable. It is a shame that she does not have anyone to take her to see *Confessions of a Pop Performer*. Maybe I can fill a gap.

'Thank you,' she says. 'It is not easy to meet peoples in London, is it?'

'It's a question of breaking the ice,' I say. 'Like so many things.'

OK, so William Shakespeare might have put it differently but it does provide the chance for me to give her arm a sympathetic squeeze and plant those luscious Lea lips on her forehead for a friendly second. Such a gesture cannot be taken exception to and may prove the springboard for more positive demonstrations of an intention to be friendly – a firm intention as percy informs me from his eyrie in my Y-fronts. Losing not a second of precious time, I kiss one of Gretchen's mince pies and zoom in fast under her hooter. Experience has taught me that this is where most judies keep their cakeholes and I am not disappointed. Gretchen's head tilts back and she stretches out her neck to push power into her kiss. Mouths are funny, aren't they? You never seem to fit quite right the first time. It is like a new pair of shoes. I draw back, give her a big smile and we try again. That's better – very nice in fact. I could be happy doing this more often. I think that Gretchen is happy too. Her body starts to shudder and she slips an arm round me and ruffles the hair at the back of my neck.

Poor kid! She probably hasn't had a Friar Tuck since she left the motherland. Time is pressing but it would be out of character if I failed to oblige. I kick the door shut behind me and quickly unzip my fly. I know that this could be considered slightly forward behaviour even in today's free and easy times but I cannot afford the extra seconds it would take me to hum the love theme from Tchaikovsky's *Romeo and Juliet*.

Gretchen lets out a little gasp as she catches a glimpse of my rampant Mad Mick and I press her to me so that its brute majesty is shut off from her eyes – you can't fault me for delicacy of feeling, can you? While I send my own mit off on a ramble up her skirt, her hesitant fingers touch and then close around the pride of the Lea fleet.

'No,' she says.

'You mean "yes",' I tell her. ' "No" means "yes" in English.'

She shakes her head sadly. 'Too big,' she says.

'Too big?' I say. I mean, it is a nice thought but I cannot allow myself to be quartered in a fool's paradise. Percy is definitely a quality article but birds don't jump out of bed and run home to mother screaming. He is just $15\frac{1}{2}$ centimetres of prime British hampton trying to do his bit for the old country – I say centimetres because everything is going metric these days, isn't it? Also, it sounds bigger.

'I no do this.'

Ah ha. I have just put my finger on the reason for the lady's statement. The entrance to her grumble is tighter than a mouse's earhole. She is a virgin. Blimey, I did not know they still made them. What a turn up for the tip of my hampton. I try and insert a digit and give up after the first squeak. I would make more progress up a valve rubber. Stick with this bird and you could have the long sensitive fingers of your dreams. Unfortunately, I do not have time to stick with the fair Gretchen. I must press on – and not up happy valley.

'I see what you mean,' I say. 'Look, I'd like to see more of you – um – seriously. What are you doing tomorrow night?'

In the end I make a date to see her at the weekend and persuade her to part with the key to 367. I hope Mrs Brown is having a bit more luck than I am and is still enjoying it. I leave Gretchen sorting out her dirty laundry in private and slip into the corridor with percy coiled reproachfully between my legs. It is not often that he gets the dish dashed from his lips like that and he is taking it badly. Almost smarting in fact.

There is no one about so I stalk down the corridor and check my equipment outside the door of 367 – my photographic equipment that is. I plan to rush in, bash off a few quick shots and scarper. I don't reckon that anyone is going to start chasing me, especially if they are in the altogether.

I listen carefully and try to remember if there was a light showing under the door when I was last here. There isn't now. No sounds either – wait a minute! A sharp exclamation and a squeak of bedsprings. They must be on the job right at this moment. Good timing, Sherlock! Just as well that I did not get to the balaclava (chaver Ed.) stage with Gretchen or I might have fallen down on the job – never a nice thing to do as we all know from bitter experience.

Taking a deep breath, I position the camera at my feet and start to insert the key in the lock like I am defusing a mine – if the tension is too much for you go out and make a cup of tea. I do hope the lock isn't stiff. I won't get much of a photo through the keyhole. I turn the key as far as it will go without meeting resistence and take another deep breath. Here we go! One two, and – bam! I turn the key, push the door open, pick up the camera and charge into the room. It is pitch dark and I stumble into a chair. Where are they?

'What the—!!??' A bloke shouts, and there is a rustle of bedclothes. I press the tit on the camera and there is a blinding flash. I press again and the bloke comes rushing at me out of the darkness – at least, I think he is coming for me. In fact, he pushes past me and dashes for the curtains. By the cringe, but he can move, that bloke! There is the sound of breaking glass and for a terrible moment I think he has chucked himself out of the window. What a love dive that would be.

Unfortunately for The Guinness Book of Records, there is a fire escape outside the window. I lean out and catch a glimpse of a bare bum through the ironwork. It is about three floors down and gathering speed like a grape rolling down a helter skelter. Thank gawd for that! Now I can scarper with a clear conscience – at least I could if some clumsy basket had not left a case in the middle of the floor. I take a purler over it and the light that clicks on in the room joins the five hundred that are flashing inside my dented nut. When I look up, Mrs Brown is kneeling on the end of the bed and trying to look at me over the top of her naked knockers. She is bristling and, believe me, she has a lot of bristol to bristle with.

'Snivelling little creep!' she hisses. 'I suppose my husband paid you to come bursting in here?'

'I don't think that Mr Brown would like me to make any comment concerning that statement,' I say, ruthlessly professional to the last.

'I could give you an albumful of photographs that would make Gordon throw a purple fit. Do you remember when the World Limbo Dancing Championships were held over here—?'

'Don't tell me,' I say. 'I have a weak heart and my doctor says that I shouldn't get over-excited.' I pick up my camera and am relieved that Mrs Brown makes no move to stop me.

'Send me a print for my collection,' she says, slumping back on the bed. 'I hope you got my best side. Why don't you take one especially for my husband?' She sticks out her tongue and extends two fingers. I raise my camera and then think better of it. Mr Brown gave few indications of being a one-man laugh riot. 'You came a couple of minutes too early. Do you know that?' Mrs Brown rotates her shoulders against the bed and draws up one of her legs so that I cop an eyeful of snatch thatch. This is obviously a very naughty lady and it is a good job that I am incorruptible. Men of lesser moral fibre might fancy their chances of filling the gap vacated by the gent now probably skipping down Baker Street in a dustbin. 'Come and sit down,' says Mrs Brown, patting the bed beside her. Her spare hand drifts down between her legs and it is soon clear that something is itching.

'I know what you want,' I say, keeping my distance.

'I was beginning to wonder,' says the lady, raising an eyebrow.

'You want to lure me close to you so that you can grab my camera and destroy the negative, don't you?' I tell her. This chick can't fool me. Dames? Huh! They think they're smart but they don't get the drop on me.

'I don't give a damn about your stupid photographs,' says the lady pleasantly. 'I want a man to finish the job. Don't say I have to wait till that dreary barman gets off duty. All he can talk about is football – even with his mouth full.'

You won't believe this but I am beginning to weaken – mentally that is. Physically, I was never straighter, stronger or longer. You have to sympathize with the woman's problem, don't you? For some of them it is like a drug. Deny them the subtle caress of the hampton and you are inflicting physical pain. I expect she is experiencing withdrawal symptoms already – very likely when you consider the speed at which that bloke left the bed.

'I do have scruples,' I say.

'Show me.' Mrs Brown places a hand on the spot where my legs join up with the rest of my body and her eyes widen.

'Uuuhm,' she purrs. 'Twelve o'clock high.'

'Look,' I say. 'You're putting me in a very difficult position.'

'Not yet I'm not,' says the evil eyeful. 'Let's start off with a few straightforward positions and build up to the difficult ones later.'

'This is very unethical,' I say, watching my zip dip floorwards. 'I'm supposed to be getting something on you.'

'What a good idea,' purrs my client's wife. 'Why don't you start with your body?' She tugs down the front of my nut hut and grabs hold of percy like she is going to pull a pint with him. What a woman. Even in repose her knockers rise up like a mountain chain.

'I might bend,' I say.

'That's bad news,' says Mrs Brown. 'I like him just the way he is.'

'I was referring to the compromising of my principles,' I say. Honestly, this bird can only think about one thing. The trouble is that she has now taken over my mind to do the thinking. I bet she put the Sex into Sexton Blake. Tinker? What she is doing to my hampton is more like a demonstration of unarmed combat.

'Come on, darling,' she coos. 'I know you're supposed to be a private dick but you don't have to be that private.'

After that I give in. I mean, anyone would, wouldn't they? With any luck I won't meet a Mrs Brown on every case. My trousers hit the floor like they have taken exception to something it said and two buttons off my shirt chip varnish off the panel above the bed. Mrs Brown folds her arms across her Manchesters and squeezes herself so tight that her eyes close and her teeth are bared – at least, that's what it looks like.

'Remember,' I say, leaping on to the bed and preparing to take up my favourite position in the inside lane. 'I'm not doing this in my professional capacity.'

## CHAPTER FOUR

In which Sid horns in and grabs the wrong end of the giggle stick with distressing consequences.

I really have to hand it to Mrs Brown – by the end of our session, there is no other way that it will get there. What a performer! If sex is food and drink to her it is no surprise that half the population of the world is starving. When I limp round to my photographer china, I hardly have the strength to push the film through his letterbox. At least, I tell myself, I have done my bit as well as Mr Brown's. The only thing that can go wrong is if the pictures don't come out. I banged them off in a hurry and I couldn't see what I was aiming at. Still, there will be something there and that should impress Sid if no one else. I think I can safely say that I have proved my ability to undertake further assignments.

The next day drags by and is not helped by Sid being in a diabolical mood because he has bashed his nut on something and is wandering about with sticking plaster all over his mug. He is not amused when I comment on the improvement and my own state of mind is not eased when my mate rings up and says that he will be pushed to get the photos to me by six. I have not told Sid about the caper because I want it to come as a complete surprise to him.

Six o'clock draws near and I pray that Mr Brown is late. Sid is only hanging on because he is waiting for the rubber to open and is having big problems with the kiddies' picture crossword he is doing.

'I don't know how they expect kids to do this,' he says.

'Lynx has four letters, doesn't it?'

I look over his shoulder. 'That's cat,' I say. 'That makes four across: cow and—'

'All right, all right, smart Alec!' says Sid. 'I can do it. It's just that they ought to get some half way decent drawings, that's all. It doesn't look like a cat with those ears. If you took that out and showed it to six kiddies in the street, they'd say lynx every time.'

'They'd say, piss off, grandad, every time,' I tell him. 'What have you got for four across? Oh Sid! It's no good squeezing calf in if there's only three spaces.'

'They could have made a mistake,' says Sid. 'I was trying to give the perisher the benefit of the doubt, wasn't I?'

It is at this instructive moment that there is a sharp tap on the door. I hope to see the outline of my mate with the photos but it is the familiar bulk of Mr Brown that eases into the office. He is looking as mean as a couple of Green Shield stamps in the middle of a collecting plate and for a horrible moment I fear that he may have cocoed that I was filing my ferret in his old lady's pleasure trove. I can just imagine him squeezing my windpipe until it could hide behind a piece of spaghetti.

'Well?' he says menacingly. It is obvious that he does not go a bundle on small talk. The BBC will have to look elsewhere for someone to introduce *Children's Choice*.

'All's well with the Noggett Investigation Bureau,' says Sid launching smoothly into his patter and raising his large magnifying glass to his eye in a gesture of greeting. Unfortunately, he has been using it as an ashtray and therefore tips ash all down the front of his whistle.

'This is for me, Sid,' I say hurriedly. 'I've been handling Mr Brown's wife – *I mean, case*!' I shriek the last three words as Mr Brown's eyes blaze and his teeth grind with a noise like someone dropping ice cubes into a glass of warm water.

'Where is the evidence?' hisses my client. 'Does this man have it?'

'Is that one question or two?' says Sid.

'The photos should be here any minute,' I say trying to get a little professional cool into my voice. 'Would you like to take a seat, Mr Brown?'

'I'm not interested in sitting!' roars Brown. 'I want results!' So saying, he drives his fist down and turns one of the office chairs into instant firewood.

'What is this?' says Sid, taking a swift step back towards the window.

'A delicate matter which I thought it favourite to attend to myself,' I say, coming into my own – well, we all do sometimes, don't we? 'This gentleman had reason to believe that his wife was deceiving him and hired us to obtain the evidence that would prove this superstition correct.'

'Where is it?' snarls Mr Brown. 'I'm a busy man. I pay for results. The sooner I can be separated from this jezebel the better!'

'Jezebel?' says Sid. 'That's a pretty name. You don't hear much of it these days, do you? Except that old Frankie Lane song. I used to reckon that. "Jezeb-e-el, Jez-e-e-eb-e-e-e".'

'Shut up!' For a moment I think that Mr Brown is going to throw a fit. I can see his Teds and half an inch of gum line. 'I poured my life into that woman and she reduces me to this! Consorting with two illiterates!'

'Watch it!' Sid draws himself up to his full height. 'If I knew what that meant, I could be offended.'

Brown buries his face in his hands. 'If I could get to grips with one of them I'd kill him. Smash him to a shapeless pulp! Is there a court in the country that would convict me?'

'I shouldn't reckon so, Squire,' says Sid soothingly. 'You wouldn't fancy a drink would you? It's from a machine but the Bovril's not bad if you like mint tea.'

I am getting worried about the non-appearance of the photographs. Mr Brown is clearly in an edgy mood and I would hate him to start dishing out the GBH in our direction. I also want to show Sid that I can bring the case to a nice smooth finale. Where are—? Oh good. Not a moment too soon either. I advance towards the bloke with the envelope as he comes through the door but am pushed aside by Sid.

'Mr Lea?' says the bloke as Sid grabs the goodies.

'They're for me,' says Sid grandly. 'These are the photographs I take it? Good. Right Mr Brown. I think you'll find you have everything you need here. Trust in NIB. I won't let you down.'

'Wait a minute, Sid!' I squawk. 'I—'

'Step aside Timothy,' says Sid moving to the desk. 'I'll handle this.'

'But Sid—'

'Not another word!' Sid holds one of his digits under my hooter and turns to Brown who is standing at his elbow like a bulldog knowing that it is feeding time. 'Excuse the impetuosity of my young assistant, Mr Brown. He gets carried away sometimes.'

'Get on with it!' grunts Brown. He grabs the side of Sid's desk and I could swear that the metal buckles.

'Hang on a minute,' says the bloke who brought the photos.

'Please!' says Sid, holding up his hand. 'This is no time for dilly dallying and idle chitchat. If the subject is of any importance we can discuss it later. At the moment there is work to be done. Mr Brown wishes to see the photographs.'

'That's what I meant,' says the bloke moving behind Brown and shaking his head violently from side to side. 'If I were you, I wouldn't—'

'Silence!' barks Sid. 'Enough! I don't know what the profession is coming to when the work of a senior sleuth is so interrupted by underlings.'

Sid spits over the front of Brown's jacket when he says senior sleuth, and there is a further interruption while it is wiped off with one of the curtains, thus making the stain permanent and pulling down the curtain rail.

'I am beginning to lose my patience!' roars Brown. 'Is it your intention to show me these photographs or is it not?'

'It is,' says Sid. 'Definitely and inconverse-uncon-in-cunt-definitely.'

While what might be described as a breathless hush falls over the room without making a sound, Sid beams into Brown's impassive face and rips open the envelope. The bloke who brought the photographs starts to edge towards the door.

'Here we are, chief,' says Sid. 'You pay for results and we provide 'em. He whips out the glossy ten-by-eights and slaps them down on the desk. Mr Brown cranes forward with Sid and me on either side of him.

Top of the pile is an unflattering portrait of a wild-eyed Sid sitting up in bed and pointing towards the camera. Mrs Brown can be clearly recognized in semiprofile, an angle that flatters her cracking set of top bollocks. She looks much nicer than Sid. Mr Brown looks from the photograph to Sid and then back to the photograph again. It is clear that a thought is occurring to him.

*'Y-o-o-u-u-u!'*

The bloke who brought the photographs starts running and I follow him through the door a close second. If there is going to be unpleasantness I wish to be no part of it.

# CHAPTER FIVE

In which Timmy and Sid are summoned to Chiltonham Ladies' College to investigate a serious case of knicker-nicking and in which Timmy pumps Françoise Fourchette, the attractive French mistress for information – amongst other things.

Sid is dead lucky because Mr Brown ruptures himself as he throws him through the wall partition. Not that he sees it like that of course. Sid has never been one to appreciate his own good fortune in moments of adversity. I feel dead choked because it is a diabolical way for things to finish when I have shown so much initiative. Trust Sid to be the stupid berk dipping his ballpoint in Mrs Brown's pinkwell.

Relations, and several different parts of the body, are strained for days after the incident and it is fortunate that I have my relationship with Gretchen to console me. Yes, the comely kraut bint – as she turns out to be – comes to the flicks with me and even wins the standout thrill of a meal at the Pizzeria – I wish they would not call it that. It makes me think of something else. I don't go a bomb on pizzas myself but they are cheap and you get scrubbed pine tables and candles thrown in for nothing. A flagon of chianti – keep the bottle for a lampshade my dear – and you are in like a dose of salts. At least usually you are. In this case I am not. It is nothing to do with the unquenchable Lea magnetism, that is as unfailing as ever. The problem lies in the area of my fair partner's snatch. It is more like a kitten than a pussy and attempts to bring percy into contact with the velvet Y meet with pain and disappointment on both sides – and particularly on the end. The whole thing – or perhaps I should say the hole thing – is doubly frustrating because Gretchen is no less than very eager to play submarine pens.

'It is so silly,' she keeps saying. 'Why am I not like other girls?'

'You are like other girls,' I tell her. 'Lots of them have this problem – at least, that's what I've heard. Sometimes if it's really bad, they go to the doctor.'

'I could not go to the doctor,' says Gretchen. 'I am not married. What would he think?'

'I expect he's come across the problem before,' I say.

Honestly, it is quite untrue that all Continental birds are ravers. A lot of them are very straitlaced. When Gretchen starts going bananas it is because her highly-sexed nature has taken over her Teutonic cool. It makes it all more exciting somehow – until the assault on the nooky cooky. It is like trying to shove your hampton up a gnat's garter.

'What are we going to do?' says the frustrated fraulein as I try and rub the circulation back into my walking out fingers. 'You are certain that it is not you who is too big?'

'Positive,' I say sadly. 'Not, of course that I'm inclined the other way, you understand? It's just one of those things. We'll have to keep working at it.'

So saying, we melt into a last passionate clinch and I bear poor confused percy away into the night. What can I do to bring Gretchen the happiness we both so richly deserve? It can't be good for my groin greyhound to keep grinding his nose into bulldog shape and Gretchen is clearly undergoing considerable frustration and physical pain. I wonder if I should write to Marjorie Proops about it?

Fortunately, I don't bring a blush to our Marje's fair cheek because another assignment crops up and thoughts of burying percy alive are driven from my mind. I check in at the office one morning and it is obvious from the expression on Sid's depraved mug that something more exciting than a change to soft bog paper in the communal lav has happened.

'Chiltonham Ladies' College,' he breathes, waving a letter under my hooter. 'This is it, Timmo. Now we're really cooking with gas. This is the big time, Bozo. Stick with me and you'll be wearing velvet Y-fronts.'

'Harm can come to a young boy through watching too much Kojak,' I tell him. 'You're going to frighten old ladies to death if you go on talking like that – and why are you eating that toffee apple?'

'They didn't have any lollipops,' says Sid. Honestly, he is just like a big soft kid sometimes. Very easily manipulated. He buys everything he sees on the telly.

'Ladies' College?' I say. 'Is that some kind of girls' school?'

'Only the best,' says Sid. 'All the birds that go there are out of the top draws. You know Princess Anne?'

I look round the room carefully. 'What have you heard?'

'Don't mess about,' says Sid. 'This could do us a lot of good. Once we get a name for being detectives to high society we could be well away. You know what they're like. They're all rotten to the cor blimey. The divorce work alone could make us a fortune.'

'You're jumping ahead a bit, aren't you?' I say. 'What's the caper?'

'Miss Craghearty reveals little in her letter,' says Sid. 'She is going to fill us in when we get to Chiltonham.'

And if ever there was a lady built to fill you in it is Miss Craghearty. One glance at her and I can see why she has MA Oxon after her name. She is built like an Aberdeen Angus with elephantiasis and her tweeds are only a slightly deeper shade of purple than her boat race. 'It is all highly distressing,' she says. 'Somebody is pilfering the gels' knicknacks. Articles of a delicate and personal nature have disappeared.'

'You mean, more knick than knack?' says Sid.

Miss Craghearty looks at Sid as if he has just crawled out of the black lagoon. 'There is an unhealthy aspect to the matter,' she observes.

'Have you been in touch with the police?' I ask.

'Absolutely not.' Miss Craghearty leans across her desk aggressively. 'We don't want any suspicion of a scandal to escape to the outside world. Chiltonham is already the butt of the media. We are constantly being subjected to scurrilous articles in the press. That is why I have sent for you. I want the whole matter cleared up in confidence. Even my own staff have not been informed of your presence.'

'Rest assured, dear lady,' says Sid. 'Discretion is our middle name. This whole distressing business will soon be no more than a painful memory. Do you suspect anybody?'

Miss Craghearty shakes her head. 'Nobody. The incidents have taken place in such circumstances that it has never been possible to point the finger at anyone.'

'Right!' says Sid with a sudden dynamism that makes me jump. 'I think that this is a case for undercover methods. With your permission, madam, I and my assistant will present ourselves in the guise of window cleaners. In that way we will be able to move around without arousing suspicion. After a few days we will have our finger on the pulse of the organisation and you can expect results to follow on swiftly.'

'Or, at the very least, clean windows,' I say cheerfully.

Miss Craghearty gives me her upper class drop dead look Mark II and Sid rises to his feet. 'We're on the job,' he says sincerely. 'You won't regret the moment you decided to come to Noggett.'

Miss Craghearty looks as if she is on the point of disagreeing with him and then follows us to the door. 'There is one thing I must ask you,' she says, dropping her voice. 'Please don't interfere with the girls' curricula.'

Sid looks at me. 'You should be saying that to him,' he says. 'He can't get enough of it. Still, never fear, good lady. I will do everything in my power to keep his unnaturally natural appetites in check.' With these words we leave Miss Craghearty looking puzzled. 'You heard what the old bag said,' says Sid as we walk down the corridor. 'If you reckoned you were going to dunk it in upper class crumpet – forget it! This is strictly business.'

Experience has shown me that arguing with Sid is like bashing your nut against the brick wall at the back of a pig pen so I say nothing. Chiltonham Ladies' College is a banquet for the mincepies and it is better to take in its natural beauties rather than indulge in agrochat. One or two natural beauties that I would not mind taking in give us the big hello from various ivy-hung windows and there is a lot of unsolicited giggling. I can see what Miss Craghearty was hinting at. These girls are obviously parched as far as contact with the one-eyed trouser snake is concerned.

'What are we looking for?' I say to Sid when we reassemble with our squeegees and scrims and a load of happy memories.

'I'm not quite certain,' says Sid. 'Miss Craghearty was obviously dead embarrassed about crashing the nitty gritty. I guess we're up against a demon knicker-nicker. Some kinky merchant is probably swanning about half-inching the birds' frillies.'

'I never fancied them so much when they were empty,' I say. 'Still, it takes all sorts, doesn't it? It would be boring if we were all the same.'

'Thank you, Jean Rook,' says Sid revealing his unpleasant sarcastic streak. 'Can you come back next week? Listen, forget the basic truths and keep your eyes open and your mits off the crumpet. If you see anything unusual, tell me. Don't try and tackle it by yourself. Is that understood?'

Half an hour later, I am sweeping the squeegee from side to side and wondering how I maintain the lithe animal grace that made me the toast of the South West London, 'I don't usually do this kind of thing, you know', set. Happy days they were. Every sharp rat tat tat promising a sharp rat, tit, tit and even more tit. Hardly a day went by when you did not fill a deep-felt need and even watching their imaginations working overtime behind the lace curtains kept the old sense of adventure razor-sharp. Many is the time I have clambered to the top of a ladder, just as I am now, and – hang on a minute. Who is that comely curve carnival stepping out of her dress? She looks a bit old to be one of the pupils. It is not just the size of her knockers but their sophisticated shape. It may be my imagination but I find that your older woman has a more refined angle of dangle in the bristol department. The young knocker rushes out to meet the world like a blancmange searching for a mould. As if activated by my interest, the unsuspecting bint advances to the mirror and cups her manchesters in her mits like she is trying to weigh them.

It is difficult to know what to do in this situation because if the bird suddenly clocks you she can get a nasty surprise and imagine that you have been having a candid gander – which, of course, you have. I usually duck out of sight and come up whistling and gazing into the top right hand corner of the window as if unaware of anything except my craft. Few women can take umbrage in such circumstances. Choosing one of the many heart-warming melodies from *Confessions of a Pop Performer* – now showing at high class cinemas throughout the length and breast of the country – I rise to the occasion feeling percy stirring like a large pink snowdrop as the first rays of spring sunshine stab the winter snow. Could this be the start of something beautiful and unexpected? Only time will tell.

Hardly have the first bars of 'Kipper, Kipper, mean as Jack The Ripper' passed thankfully from my lips than the bird spins round. One glance in my direction and her boat race registers extreme surprise followed by consternation and then anger. Before I can imitate crisp morning sunshine with my teds she has thrown up the window and delivered a couple of right handers in the area of the middle mush. Not content with this violent attack on my chat feature, she then attempts to push the ladder away from the window. Highly unpleasant for Timothy, I am certain you will agree. It could be The House of Commons instead of a posh birds' school.

'Cut it out!' I holler, warding off the bird's flailing mits. 'What's the matter with you? I'm the window cleaner, aren't I?' I wave my squeegee in front of the bird's snoz and slowly, very slowly, her expression changes.

'Oh no!' she says. 'I am so sorree! I think you are— oh it is too 'orrible!' And with those few words in a very froggy accent, she bursts into tears.

In such a situation few can beat my speed over the first hundred yards and my leg is over the windowsill before you can say 'Roger Carpenter with a double rupture'. 'Don't cry,' I say. 'I know what you thought. You thought I was him didn't you? Well, I'm not. I'm me. Timothy Lea. I can't really say anything but I know a bit more than I can let on about. Know what I mean?'

The bird shakes her head sadly. 'I sink I make a big mistake to come 'ere. My Engleesh is not good enough. I no understand anything.'

'You teach here, do you?' I ask. 'You're the French mistress, are you?' French Mistress. The very words trip off the tongue like 'frilly panties'. I hardly like to say them unless my imagination books an appointment with the four fingered widow.

'Assistant French Mistress,' says the bird, 'Françoise Fourchette. I am sorree that I 'it you.'

'Don't worry,' I say. 'It happens all the time. The girls giving you trouble, are they?'

'It is not that,' says Françoise. 'I 'ate work and I love sick.' It is not often that a bird puts the mockers on my powers of rabbit but on this occasion I am rendered well and truly speechless. These Continental birds have some funny ways and no mistake. I knew a bloke who fancied the smell of his own farts but he was not in this class. 'I should never have left 'im,' continues the lovely Mademoiselle Fourchette. ' 'E was part of me.'

It occurs to me that I may have mistaken the lady's drift.

'Oh, love-sick!' I say. 'You fancy some bloke back home, do you?' I know that it is one of the many nasty things about me but once a bird starts blubbing, my cock becomes rock and I feel like bashing her over the pudenda with it. People are always rabbiting on about how sex should be a manifestation of love, respect and tenderness but I don't reckon so much myself – I mean, it can be all those things, but it can be a lot of other things as well. It depends on your mood, the direction of the wind, what you had for supper and whether her Mum is likely to be back late from the bingo.

'Pierre,' she says. ' 'E supplied so many of my needs. But why do I tell you this thing? You 'oo are a complete stranger.'

'Sometimes complete strangers are the best people to help,' I say. 'Outsiders can see things more clearly. If you think about something too much, your point of view becomes distorted.'

Something else that is becoming distorted is the front of my overall. Percy is signalling his desire to prove that actions speak louder than words and is beginning to thrash about like a manic garden hose. He senses, as I do, that Françoise is in need of the remedial balm of the magic poundabout and is in no mood to hang about – very wise too. If you are a dick, hanging about is the worst way of proving your point.

'This terrible man,' she says. 'It is 'orrible. I am so frightened.'

She starts to cry again and I feel that the least I can do is give her a comforting pat on the shoulder – well, not so much the shoulder, more the upper arm: where it joins the interesting bits – the threepenny bits. To my surprise she suddenly grips my hand and squeezes it tight. 'There, there,' I say – it is ridiculous because she must know where it is.

'You know,' she says slowly. 'I think most of all I am frightened by myself. I 'ate this man yet at the same time I want 'im – I need 'im. There is a part of me that cries out for 'im. I am – 'ow you say—? Frustrée?'

'Frustrated,' I say, allowing my voice to sink a couple of octaves into its best bedside manner. 'I know how you feel. It must be difficult when you're a long way from 'ome – I mean, home.' The whole case is taking on psychological overtones, isn't it? I don't usually reckon it much myself. I read a book about it once, appropriately enough by a French geezer – Simen On, I think his name was, probably of Chinese extraction – but I couldn't get into it. Everybody was barring their doors and muttering behind closed shutters. Nothing ever happened and the bloke who did it knotted himself because he thought his budgerigar didn't love him. Blooming stupid really. I prefer action to plot: Half a dozen murders, a couple of crooked cops, three car chases and the snooty bird who did it all, copping the hero and thirty years in Sing Sing in the last chapter.

As I recall it, there was no sex in Monsieur On's work – apart from the bloke's feelings towards his budgie, and they were not requited, bird lovers will be relieved to know. In the present situation I reckon I can improve on that. With this outspoken lady seriously contemplating a spot of in and out with a criminal and pining for her Pierre it is clearly my beholden duty to slip her a length. What is a private eye if he is not a doctor trying to cure society's ills? I will acknowledge all answers to that question written on the back of a five pound note. Of course, it has nothing to do with finding the demon knicker nicker but you can't have everything. I will take things one at a time and try not to get flustered.

'I'd better close the window, hadn't I?' I say. This is what I have heard called a rhetorical question and is delivered with a side order of heavy overtone. I always reckon that French birds are a sight more sophisticated than our homespun lovelies and less likely to respond to a straightforward request for a trial sample of conjugal rights. It is also a case of 'the least said, soonest amended'. If you feed a bird a series of casual throwaways which bear little relation to each other she can put any interpretation on them she likes. By the time she finds out what you were really getting at – you've got to it.

I slam down the window and turn to face Françoise. She looks into my eyes and I look into hers. She is wearing a mustard-coloured slip and her lower lip trembles – I don't think that the two events are connected.

'Let me help you,' I say. I stretch out my arms and hope that she does something – you feel such a berk if she doesn't. The only way out is to launch into a fishing story.

'Thees ees madness,' she says. 'I am so ashamed. I do not know what comes over me.'

'Nobody will ever know,' I say. 'It will be our secret.'

If only I could play the violin I would really be in business. I can seen that Françoise is hesitating and you know what they say about people who hesitate – up shit creek without adequate means of propulsion.

'Come here,' I say.

Françoise takes a faltering step towards me and her fate is sealed as if by an epoxy resin. I snatch her into my arms and her small cupid's bow mouth comes up to mine like a swing boat on its upward sweep. I engulf her lips and send my brewer's bung on a journey into the interior. She quivers in my arms and settles on to my cakehole like a baby to the teat. What suction power! Even at this stage in our relationship I can sense myself in the presence of a lady who likes to suck. I mould her to my frame and help myself to a handful of haunch. A beautiful piece of equipment it is too. Filling every contour of the palm. Swiftly, my eager fingers hitch up the slip and pleasure themselves on the silken fabric beneath. The same material as the slip at a guess. And where – I hear you ask – is percy while all this is going on? Not far away. Climbing swiftly and silently up the front of my Y-fronts. Growing in size and eagerness with every inch. Trembling with ill-suppressed longing. Françoise breaks off our kiss and shows me her teeth as she spreads her hand across the front of my trousers.

'I love 'im,' she husks. There is a plaintive edge to her voice but I am not certain whether she is talking about boyfriend Pierre or my own special favourite – Passionate Percy, the orginator of the drainpipe trouser.

'I know,' I say, reckoning that these two simple words will serve in either eventuality.

I waste no further time on sweet talk but send five matelots to board her knickers. They swarm over the side with a speed and sense of purpose that Blackbeard the Pirate would have admired and plunge into the juiceville like a warrenful of feeding bunnies hitting their burrows as they hear Farmer Brown approaching with his bang-stick. In fact, of course, it is not Farmer Brown but Timothy Lea who represents the real danger as far as bang sticks are concerned. You need a firearm licence to carry what I have between my legs at the moment and Twentieth Century Fox searchlights make a worse job of combing the sky. I set my lips on collision course for the fanciable frog's cakehole and pull down her panties so that there is no danger of the elastic stopping the circulation in my wrist. It is clear that she is eager for a pork banger in her hanger because she is shivering like a carton of gnat's wings in a force nine gale and making noises that you never hear on the BBC French for Schools Programme. She sits back on the bed and peels off her panties and tights like she is trying to break a record for doing it – it could be the British All-Comers as far as me and my throbbing friend are concerned. I don't hang about but shed my threads and allow her to cop an eyeful of proud perce bobbing up and down like a roundabout horse. The sight obviously grabs her because she repays the compliment and seizes my hampton in one of her dainty mits.

'Come,' she says.

I am certain she does not mean that and this supposition is reinforced when she leads me towards a washbasin in the corner of the room. What does she have in mind? I am not used to being taken for walkies by my Mad Mick. To my surprise she turns on the hot tap and smiles at me reassuringly.

'Wait for it to warm up,' she says.

She need not worry. At the moment, a drop of ice cold water on my knob would turn to steam on impact. Satisfied, with the temperature, Françoise pops in the plug, half fills the basin, turns off the tap, works up a nice rich lather – I don't reckons Katie Boyle would fancy it on her mug after this lot – and slaps it on my love joint. Dead hygienic the frogs obviously. Either that or she has a shrewd suspicion about some of the places my giggle stick has been. I kiss her while she is doing it and she gets so carried away that she puts her soapy hands round my naked body and digs her finger nails into my shoulders. Dead sexy I find that.

I start pulling her towards the bed and she snatches for a towel and tries to dry me off before we make a dent in the counterpane. I slip my hand between her legs and play the opening bars of Tchaikovsky's First Piano Concerto on her snatch. I don't know if she has an ear for classical music but her grumble obviously responds to the magic of the maestros. Her mouth drops open and she draws up her legs and squeezes my hampton like she is using it to haul herself out of a bath. I tiptoe away in the middle of my favourite passage and start to tug up her slip. Her bristols strain expectantly against the semi-see-through fabric of her light blue bra and I brush aside the barrier and set my lips to raise gherkins where once only strawberries would grow.

Françoise squeaks with pleasure as I pamper her knockers and for a few minutes she wears her slip like a halter. Then she rises up and with a quick scissor snap of arm movement, sheds slip and bra before kissing my neck and setting off on a snail trail southwards. Her moist lips guide her flickering tongue down towards the site of her previous handiwork and I feel percy quiver – I would say stiffen, but this hampton can't get any stiffer. Françoise reaches my derby kell and her tongue slops into my belly button like it is a pool caught by an advancing tide. Her right hand is ranging the length of my hampton from its lighthouse tip to the root deep between my legs and I feel like space control waiting to put a couple of million quid's worth of rocket into space. Françoise's shell-like earhole settles against the upper reaches of my pubes and 'Oh!' closely followed by 'Eeeeh!!!' and then 'Aaaaaaaargh!!!' Ecstasy is too small a word for what is happening to fortunate percy. This foreign lady must be an exponent of the French horn to judge by her virtuoso performance at crutch level. I lay back and enjoy a couple of quiet movements – and then one or two rather noisy movements as Françoise speeds up her finger action.

'Easy!' I say. 'Easy!!! – AAARGH!!!'

For a moment it is touch and go – in fact it is very nearly touch and gone – then I decide that the time has come to take the initiative. After all, I am representing Great Britain again and you can't just lie there, can you? Selecting a moment when Mademoiselle Fourchette has paused to brush the hair from her pretty brown minces, I draw her up to my body and give her gateau-hole a taste of the two horizontal strips of pink flesh that nestle under my hooter. When I have stirred this feature up a bit, I press the lady down firmly against the counterpane and windscreen wipe my north and south across her bristols pausing at the end of each sweep to nibble her knocker knobs. This treatment obviously goes down well so my cakehole follows suit and travels south to muffshire. Hardly have I crossed the furry frontier than the expectant quiver turns into a fleshquake. Françoise's middle third bounces up and down like a pen of kangaroos sensing Naafi break and I have to press my mits firmly on her belly before giving tongue to a much appreciated love yodel. Her looks and lingers tangle with my barnet and for a moment I think that she is trying to turn me into instant Kojak.

Percy is now double eager to hit the clit slit so I disengage my cakehole and position my frisky friend within stabbing distance of the target area. A preliminary thrust and Mademoiselle Fourchette takes the matter firmly in hand and pockets my socket rocket like she is on piecework in the packaging department of a cigar factory.

'Ooh la la!' she says in a tone of pleased surprise, and proceeds to thump out the theme from Ravel's Bolero. What a groover! Lots of Swiss watches have vastly inferior movements.

What she is doing to me makes me think of those telly commercials where you see an enormous vat of toffee being stirred. Thick and rich and creamy – I'll have to stop or I'll pour myself over my honeycomb centres.

I harness myself to the lady's irresistible motion and slowly begin to build in a dimension of added thrust – for me, it is like canoeing down a fast flowing stream. I have to keep going faster than the current or I can't maintain control of the boat. I slide my hands under the bird's sit feature and feel her beautifully sculpted back knockers curve within the contour of my palms. Now I can really concentrate my artillery barrage on the area where it is going to be most effective. Bang, bang, bang, pause. Bang, bang, bang, pause. Increasing the weight of the stroke each time I engage with my pocket howitzer and seek out Françoise's north and south for the tender attention of my cakehole. As we kiss, I feel her flinching before the expected onslaught of my hampton and after each stroke she gives a triumphant roll like a swimmer riding the buffet of heavy waves. Fortunately for the future of Anglo-French relations it is becoming increasingly clear that we are approaching the moment of truth in tandem. Françoise's moans and groans are becoming more frequent and demanding and I am finding it difficult to restrain percy's impulse to indulge in a cream scream. Three more dynamic thrusts and my new friend opens her mouth so wide that I can see what she had for breakfast. She digs her mits into the cleft between my back bumpers and pulls so hard that for a second I think she is going to split me down the middle of the orchestras. I bury my head in the pillow beside her neck and turn percy into a piece of equipment that could lay a stream of rivets along the side of the QE2. A sensation of warmth sweeps through my loins and hesitates for a few delicious seconds before thundering the length of my hampton and exploding with a force that lifts Françoise six inches up the bed. I don't understand what she is saying but I guess that it must mean the same thing in any language.

'Hello? Miss Fourchette? Mademoiselle Fourchette, are you there?'

My blood turns colder than a penguin's chuff in a blizzard. The voice is coming from outside the door but the doorknob is turning. I leap from the bed and feel my knees buckle as I hit the carpet. I snatch up a pair of pants – but that is all I have time to snatch up. The door opens and I find myself face to face with Miss Craghearty. She stares at me in amazement and then starts back in horror when she sees what I have in my hand – Françoise's panties.

## CHAPTER SIX

In which an unfortunate misunderstanding causes Timmy to flee to the gym and become painfully and athletically involved with Imogen, Natasha, Titania, Grizelda and the making of the school blue film.

It is then that I do something silly. I think it may be as a result of leaping about so soon after an energetic bout of in and out. A short breather is always favourite after saying goodbye to a few hundred thousand old friends. Anyway, I suddenly get the idea that I must stop Miss Craghearty recognising me and, to this end, pull Françoise's panties over my nut. Squinting out of one leg hole, I brush past Miss Craghearty – at a guess, the nearest she has got to sexual intercourse in fifty years – and burst into the corridor. I am heading down it at about a hundred and forty miles an hour when I hear the high-pitched chatter of female voices approaching round a corner. A sharp right turn brings me up against a door marked 'Matron' and I bung it open and dart inside. Sitting on a chair is Sid and across his lap a large blonde bird wearing a nurse's uniform, the skirt of which is up round her waist. She scrambles to her feet as the door opens – and practically scrambles Sid's Mad Mick as well if the expression on his boat race is anything to go by. I don't hang about to dictate a congratulations telegram but piss off back the way I have come. Most of this is now filled by Miss Craghearty carrying a pike she has obviously lifted from one of the walls. While I jibber in terror and leap about ten feet in the air the old bag lunges at my cluster like she is training to be a park keeper. With an evasive skill that any cabinet minister would envy I dodge Dracula's mother and half fall down a flight of stairs. Behind me I can hear Miss Craghearty's shouts of 'Scrag the bounder!' augmented by a chorus of shrill shrieks and excited screams and the pounding of hundreds of pairs of girlish feet. I must escape! The Noggett Investigation Bureau will never recover from the shame of its star detective being discovered stark bollock naked with a pair of women's knicks over his nut. Even Sherlock Holmes would be pushed to give a satisfactory explanation.

I pick myself up at the bottom of the stairs and blunder towards two doors directly in front of me. Perhaps they give out on to the grounds. Through the rhododendrons, over the wall and I will be free. Just a question of finding someone who gives lifts to stark naked hitch hikers. But the doors do not give out on to the grounds. As I burst through them I find myself in the middle of a group of birds wearing blue serge panties and white singlets – though they would be better off with doublets most of them. Even in my hunted condition I cannot help noticing that I am in the presence of a veritable knocker harvest. I am also in a gymnasium. There are ropes, vaulting horses, horizontal bars and all that clobber. As the birds squeal and cluster round me, I try to adjust my knickers and look wholesome.

'You've got to help me,' I say. 'There's been a misunderstanding. I'm being chased but I haven't done anything.'

Frankly, I don't reckon that anyone is going to go a bundle on offering me a helping mit but in this respect I could not be more wrong. The birds grab a long gander at the lustre of my cluster and their eyes light up.

'He looks all right to me,' says a redhead with two cracking reasons for saving money on Ostermilk. 'What do you say, Imogen?'

'Definitely!' says a blonde wand with a chassis like the golden years of British motoring. 'I say into the horse with him immediately. Rally round, gels!'

Before you can say Roger Carpenter, the birds have lifted the top three layers of the horse and I have got my leg over the remaining two – sides, not girls.

'Ta a million,' I say. 'I'll never be able to thank you enough.'

'Don't bank on it,' says the bird addressed as Imogen.

Before I can concentrate on the exact meaning of her words, the top clamps down and my only view of the outside world is obtained through one of the lifting slits on the side of the horse. Hardly have I disappeared from view than Miss Craghearty bursts into the gym with about forty kids at her heels like beagles.

'Have you seen anything?' she croaks. 'There's a naked sex maniac loose in the building. He's wearing a-a-a pair of short bloomers on his head.'

'Did he have any distinguishing features?' says a voice that I recognise as belonging to Imogen.

Miss Craghearty clearly does not warm to this remark. 'This is no time for facetiousness, Imogen,' she says coldly. 'This is undoubtedly the man we have been waiting for. He will stop at nothing to work his filthy willy – I mean, wiles. Be on your guard. If you see anything untoward, raise the alarm.'

'We will, Miss Craghearty,' chants a chorus of dutiful female voices. 'He won't get past us.'

'Practising for the display?' says Miss Craghearty, relaxing a little. 'Good show! That's the stuff to give the troops. Very well, I'll leave you to it. Keep up the good work. Remember the school motto: Floreat Chiltona.'

A door slams on a rush of teenage tootsies and I begin to breathe easier. If I can lay my hands on a few articles of clothing in the changing room I may be able to get out more or less threaded. What nice helpful girls I have stumbled upon – but why aren't they letting me out?

'Titania's fetching her camera,' is the reply I get when I proffer the question. 'It's awfully good. It's got an exposure meter – jolly appropriate, don't you think?'

'Camera?' I pant. 'What do you want a camera for?'

'The school blue film,' says a chick with two of the nicest pins you could ever hope to find steering your hampton into a cool de sac. 'We got fed up with shooting bank raids on the science labs. Do you know how much *Emmanuelle* has grossed? It's pretty awful too. It takes place in Bangkok and there is sod all banging and absolutely no cock.'

'Very funny,' I say. 'Now can I come out? I'll leave you to get on with practising for your display.'

'You can forget our display, you fiend,' says Imogen tenderly. 'We want to broaden our horizons. It's not often we come face to face with a real life sex maniac.'

'What a heavenly thought,' says another bird wistfully.

'Hang on a minute,' I say. 'I wasn't kidding, you know. I'm as normal as the bloke next door.'

'We don't have a bloke next door,' says Imogen. 'That's part of the trouble – ah, here comes Titania. Is the coast clear, Tits?'

The aptly nick-named knocker factory nods her head and the rest of her body shudders in sympathy. 'Shagnasty has taken her posse off towards the pav,' she says. 'We should be able to get a few feet in the can before high tea. Have you outlined the plot yet?'

'We'll make that up later,' says Imogen. 'All we want now is the filthy bits. Let's get on with it while the light lasts.'

'We drunk all the light during rehearsals,' says a judy,

taking the top off a medicine ball and revealing that it is an ice bucket. 'You'll have to make do with gin.'

'It's not the stuff the lower fourth distilled, is it?' says Titania. 'I dissolved my dutch cap in that.'

'Look,' I say. 'You've got the wrong end of the giggle stick. I'm not the bloke who's been knicking the nickers.'

'Then how do you know he exists?' says Imogen triumphantly.

'Well,' I say. 'I – er—'

'Why do you do it?' says Titania. 'Can you explain the nature of the thrill you get?'

'Oh, shut up Tits!' says Imogen. 'We're not doing this for the BBC. We haven't even got sound. Let's get cracking with the uncomfortable-making bits.'

'Right ho,' says Titania. 'You keep cave, Tara. Off with the lid, gels.'

The top of the horse comes off and I straighten up and try to rub some circulation back into my cramped limbs. The birds gaze at me with an interest that I find slightly unnerving and I deem it advisable to be on my way. 'Thanks a bunch, ladies,' I say. 'I won't forget what you've done for me. I was in a tight spot back there—'

'Good,' says Imogen. 'You're going to need all your experience. Grab him girls!'

Before I can open my mouth to shout for help, eager hands seize me and I find myself spreadeagled across the vaulting horse with my limp dick drooping towards the coconut matting. Imogen has a worried expression on her face.

'That's hopeless,' she says. 'Surely you can do better than that? After all, you are a professional.'

'We could stick an indian club between his legs,' says Titania.

Imogen shakes her head scornfully. 'With a couple of

medicine balls on either side of it? No, it would notice in the close-ups. I can't abide dissimulation. With me it's the real thing or nothing. Dicky pricky makes me sicky.'

'I suppose there's only one thing for it,' says a chick with lips like miniature air beds.

'You mean, get another one?' says a droopy redhead. 'That's what Mummy always does.'

'We haven't got time,' says Titania. 'We'll have to make do with what we've got. OK Natasha. You can suck a Polo Mint for longer than any other girl in the school.'

'Girls, please!' I gasp as melon mouth licks her lips and takes a purposeful step towards me. 'Do you realise what you are doing? What about the age of consent?'

'You passed that years ago,' scoffs Imogen. 'You'll have to think of a better one than that.'

'Not me – you!' I shriek. 'I could get ten years for what you're about to do to me.'

'Don't worry about that,' says Titania. 'We're the mature sixth. We're only staying on because Shagnasty wants to win the inter-schools gymnastic competition. Right, Natasha, make great oaks from little acorns grow. Grizelda, up on the wall bars. Imogen, can you get it all in?'

'I think so,' says Imogen starting to pull her panties down. 'I'd better have a trial run though.'

'I was referring to the picture!' scolds Titania delivering a stinging slap on the wrist. 'You wanted to be camera-woman, didn't you? I suppose now you want the Linda Lovelace role?' I am beginning to worry about Grizelda. Why is she climbing up the wall bars with that rope in her hands? She couldn't be intending to – no! It's impossible. If she missed it could be finis for my penis.

'A-a-a-argh!' I say. 'O-o-o-o-h! Wha-a-a-a-t are yo-u-u-u-OOOOOOOOOOOOH!!!' I wish I could be more specific but it is difficult to concentrate with Natasha inflating my love joint – from 'lie-low' to 'lilo' in fact.

Titania reads the terror behind the ecstasy in my eyes.

'It's all right,' she says. 'I'm going to cut, the moment that Grizelda swings away from the wall bars. We'll pick her up enjoying the fruit of your loins.' I nod gratefully. For a moment I thought that it was me they were going to have to pick up. 'OK Natasha, hold it' snaps Titania. 'You're not getting a prize for it. Let's see what we've got going for us. Hhmm, not bad. It's pointing in the right direction anyway. OK Immers. Crash off a few shots in case it wilts. Natasha, stand by with your lips. Harriet, get the rings ready.'

'The rings?' I gulp.

'Yup.' Imogen begins to wax lyrical. 'It's going to look absolutely super. You're hanging upside down with your legs through the rings and Peta is spread-eagled against the wall bars. You zoom down and – eh voila! Just like two bats mating.'

Or one poor bastard getting a U-bend in his hampton, I think to myself. Why couldn't they get Robin Askwith to play my part – or, better still, my parts?

'Don't you think it's all a bit complicated?' I say. 'Not to mention dangerous.'

'We don't know the meaning of the word fear,' says Imogen. It just shows what a lousy education you get at these private schools, doesn't it? And no prizes for guessing why they call them private. These bints clearly never think about anything else.

'Look,' I say. 'I want to get something straight.'

'Natasha has already got it lovely and straight,' says Titania. 'You could draw isoceles triangles with it if you wanted.' So saying, the wicked wench runs her fingers along the length of my hampton like she is playing a scale on it.

'Maybe we should shoot it as it comes,' says Imogen wistfully.

'Oh we will, darling,' says Titania. 'That's going to be the climax of the film – if you'll excuse the expression.'

'I think you misunderstand me,' says Imogen. 'I was referring to continuity not content. Once I've got Grizelda launching herself from the wall bars we might as well snap off a few shots of her in the saddle.'

'Oh su-u-u-pa!' squeaks Grizelda who is by no means an undelectable bit of totty. 'Hey ho, Slaver away!'

'It's "Hey ho, Silver, away!"' corrects Titania. 'Still, in your case you may be right. Wipe away that drool and let's make movies. Are you ready, Imogen? Right, roll 'em.'

'We're not stopping for a joint now, are we?' says Grizelda sounding really broken up. 'Golly, what a swizz. Just when it was getting to an interesting bit.'

'I was referring to the camera, you fool!' hisses Titania. 'Honestly, you're so stupid, Grizelda. I don't know why I gave you such a large part.'

'It's just ordinary, really,' I say.

'It's because Grizelda let you eat all her tuck,' says Natasha reproachfully. 'When I gave you my gatefold of Burt Reynolds showing his all you said I was going to get it.'

'Shut up, both of you!' says Imogen. 'Shagnasty is going to be back in a minute and we haven't done anything.'

'Right!' says Titania. 'Ready Grizelda? Open your legs and try and look like a gel who's about to impale herself on half a foot of ecstasy. Stand by for the cunt-down. On three. One-two-three!'

Grizelda reveals a snatch like a fur lumber jacket and launches herself into space. She skims inches over my hampton and the vibration alone sends a tinkle through my tonkle. Thank goodness we are faking the action shots.

'Did you get it?' says Titania addressing Imogen. 'Right, print it – and don't go to Boots this time.'

'Now for the tender love interest,' coos Grizelda tossing aside her rope and starting to scramble astride my thighs. 'I reckon this beats mixed hockey any day.'

'Back, you impetuous fool!' scolds Titania. 'What in the name of Norman Cohen do you think you're doing? Have I given you your motivation yet?'

'I don't know,' says Grizelda. 'I thought it was just a case of climbing on to his naughty part and joggling up and down a bit.'

'Joggling up and down a bit!' says Titania scornfully. 'No wonder people say that cinema is dead in this country. Where's the unsullied art in that? Thank goodness I'm here to lend a little style and dignity to the proceedings. I didn't see *Confessions of a Window Cleaner* forty-six times for nothing, you know.'

'I thought you did,' says Natasha. 'You told me that the manager gave you a free pass after you'd given him a blow—'

'Must we go into the tedious details?' says Titania wearily. 'Step aside and I'll show you how I want this scene played. Natasha, make with the molars. The star of our movie is making droopy instead of whoopy.'

It is true that all the chat has caused percy to start dropping off but a quick touch of the Hoover Constellations from Natasha – call me 'Jaws', folks – soon has my happy hampton pointing out the moon to his bum buffers. Oh, the agony of it all. Pinned against a vaulting horse by half a dozen knock-out nymphets whilst number seven satisfies her nunga hunger and number eight peels off her panties and starts doing limbering up exercises. Nip outside and shout for help, will you? – hang on! I was only kidding.

'It's a rotten swizz,' sulks Grizelda. 'You're going to do this all the time. We're never going to get a look in.'

'That's right,' agrees Imogen. 'What chance have I got, stuck behind this camera?'

There is an ugly murmur of agreement and Titania waves her arms in the air in frustration. 'Crumbs!' she says. 'I suppose everybody wants to direct this sequence? Marvellous, isn't it? It's my camera, too.'

'Well you use it then and I'll direct,' says Imogen trying to push the camera into Titania's arms and take off her knicks at the same time.

'Hold it – not his thing, Natasha! Honestly you are a twit! I'm glad we don't have a clapper board. Back the lot of you. I'm having first go!' So saying, Titania straddles my thighs and wriggles forward until my action man kit is threatening to activate her trip switch. I struggle manfully – well, I readjust my bum in a more comfortable position – and prepare to take her quimper without a whimper. Titania seizes my hampton like it might sting her if she did not grab it hard enough and stuffs it away in the first place you would look if you were playing hide and seek. 'Now,' she says. 'Now-oo-oh-OH! This is what I want you to do, Grizzy-oooooh!'

'Are we making a sex film or a documentary on bronco busting?' says Imogen tartly. 'Do stop hopping up and down, Titters. His eyes are beginning to glaze over.'

'Shall I pull the knickers over his head again?' says Natasha grabbing Mademoiselle Fourchette's panties.

'He's not a parrot!' scolds Titania. 'Stop flapping all of you! I know what I'm doing.'

'I know what you're doing, too, and I want to do it!' protests Grizelda. She gives Titania a push and within seconds the whole lot of them are thumping each other. Mighty taxing on the hampton it is too. Titania is determined not to be displaced and she is exerting considerable leverage on my whelk stirrer. 'Girls, please!' I gasp. 'Control yourselves!' My protests are silenced by some chick who decides that she wants to kiss me. While she rearranges my lips, Titania continues to bounce up and down on my hampton and it becomes clear that I am about to be taken out of myself. The situation is not helped by an unseen pair of hands that start massaging my orchestras. That really puts the kibosh on it. A damsel's digits delicately dusting my Maltesers has never failed to winkle forth the liquid pearl.

'Y-a-a-a-rgh!' I yodel – or it might have been 'W-a-a-a-u-u-ugh!' I can't really remember – 'Geronimo!'

My one shout ricochets off all four walls of the gym and silence falls faster than a South East Asian government. 'Now look what you've done!' accuses Imogen. 'You've blown it.'

'I brew it, she blew it,' says Titania, nodding towards Natasha. 'Oh dear, what a shame. You are a naughty boy, aren't you? No staying power.'

'It's all your fault,' grumbles Imogen. 'You did that on purpose so that we couldn't have a go.'

'Nonsense!' snaps Titania, slipping out of the saddle and pulling on her panties. 'Back to your positions and let's make movies! We'll do the rings sequence and then go on to the roller skates.'

'Hang on a minute!' I gasp. 'What's with the roller skates? I'm already complaining to EQUITY.'

'It's going to be lovely,' says Titania, getting all excited again. 'I got the idea from watching ice dancing. It's very nice but it needs another dimension to make it really come to life.'

I begin to have an unpleasant suspicion about what may be coming next. 'You mean, the couples actually—?'

'Couple. Yes, dear heart. Ice copulation that's what we're going to call it. Imagine a couple of pirouettes, two spin turns and then ending up on his thing. All to Swan Lake. It must be the most exciting sporting event you've ever seen mustn't it?'

'They'll be fascinated down at the accident clinic,' I tell her. 'Frankly I think that "Grandstand On Ice" would be a better name for it.'

Titania ignores my little joke. 'It's a pity about the ice,' she says. 'Still, it will probably be easier to perfect the movements on roller skates.'

'And not getting frostbite of the hampton will be a bonus, as well,' I say. Honestly, some birds don't care, do they? Once they get an idea in their heads, they are not interested in tedious little details like whether your giggle stick ends up as the first flesh-flavoured ice lolly. 'I'm afraid I'm going to have to put my foot down,' I say.

'I'm afraid you're going to have to put it up,' says Titania firmly. 'Don't let him escape, gels!' Before I can take a step towards the door I am seized and held upside down while my legs are thrust through two metal rings at the end of a couple of ropes. 'Let me go!' I screech. 'Why are you doing this? Have you got it in for me?'

'Not yet,' breathes Imogen. 'But I will do as soon as we've done this long shot.'

'Haul him up to the ceiling,' commands Titania. 'I'll tell you when to let go.'

'His thing is looking in pretty poor shape,' says Natasha. 'Do you think I ought to—'

'Down, Fang!' says Titania. 'You won't see it in this

shot he'll be coming down so fast. Maybe the rush of cool air will put some mettle in it.'

I start to whimper but I am wasting my breath. These girls are as heartless as I am shortly to be partless. A rope is flung over a beam and I am hauled up so that I am in the position of a trapeze artist about to be released on his downward swing. The floor seems about a hundred feet below and I am parallel to it. If my legs slip out of the rings I will be a gonner. As it is, I have a good chance of picking up a hooter full of splinters – very handy if I want to pick my teeth with my nose.

'Ready, Immers?' Titania sounds as posh as the Meals on Wheels lady and I would love to treat her to a bunch of fives up her upper class bracket. Imogen squats by the door of the gym and squints through her aperture – it's all right, she doesn't have to be double-jointed to do it.

'Fine,' she says. 'Arabella, shin up a rope and prepare to release Batman.'

'Don't you mean Robin?' I say, game to the last. 'I feel more like a bloody bird in this position.'

'Do you want me to pull the knickers over his head?' says Arabella who has made a fair job of shinning up the rope. 'I thought he looked rather groovy when he came in.' She gives my goolies a playful tweak and I recognise the fingers that were partly responsible for the damp patch on top of the vaulting horse.

Titania looks thoughtful. 'Hhhhm,' she says. 'I don't usually expect to receive advice from the camera crew but I must concede that you have a point which, incidentally, is more than our star seems to have at the moment. The symbolism appeals to me. The hooded falcon escaping from the wrist and blindly hurling itself into space. It adds a totally new dimension to our movie: sex with a message.'

I am just about to tell her that as far as I am concerned

the message is 'HELP!' when the door bursts open and Tara rushes in. 'Cave!' she shrieks. 'Shagnasty is coming this way. Scoot everybody!'

'Hold your ground!' orders Titania sternly. 'The first girl to panic forfeits her turn with the house turnip. If we carry on as if we were practising, everything will be all right. Shaggers is as blind as a bat.'

'It's no good,' gasps Arabella. 'I can't hold him much longer. He's slipping away from me!'

'What are you holding him by, you fool?' says Titania, beginning to sound alarmed. 'We've got a lot more close-ups to do, you know.'

'She's coming!' squeaks Tara.

Even as the door bursts open I feel Arabella's grip on my heels slacken – yes, it is my heels, Lea-lovers. The wicked ha'porth has pulled the panties over my nut but I don't need extrasensory perception to know that I am about to take off – that's a joke, isn't it? The only thing I have left to take off is the sticking plaster on my left elbow.

'H-e-e-e-lp!!' I scream as I sail through the air. It's not going to help but it makes me feel better.

'What ON – UGH!!!' Miss Craghearty is probably not aware of it but she has just copped the world's highest muff dive. I know because I can taste the tweed through Francoise's panties. My legs have come out of the rings so I scramble to my feet – luckily I don't have far to scramble because they are just beside me – and start belting down the corridor.

It gets a bit hectic sometimes but I do lead a rich and varied life.

# CHAPTER SEVEN

In which Timmy takes Gretchen home to meet Mum and Dad – and regrets it.

'The butler did it,' says Sid.

'The butler?' I say.

'Yes,' says Sid. 'It's an open and shut case. Like your Dad when he's helping himself to a fag without passing them around. He was run down by a trolley full of sugar outside Sainsbury's.'

'Dad?' I say.

Sid shakes his head impatiently. 'No! The butler. When they loosened his collar they found that he was wearing half a dozen stretch bras. He had three pairs of flower patterned panties under his pin stripes.'

'That's amazing,' I say. 'I didn't even know that the school had a butler.'

'It doesn't,' says Sid. 'He was on loan from one of the local nobs. Supposed to clean the silver and help with the flower arrangements. Fate intervened just as I was about to expose him.'

'What a pity,' I say. 'I expect he would have liked that. If it's not a rude answer – how did you tumble him?'

Sid looks pleased with himself. 'It was the matron. She put me on to it.'

'Oh yes,' I say, suppressing a smile. 'How?'

'Well,' says Sid. 'It was only a little thing.'

'I can believe that,' I say, having another secret chortle. 'You had to pump her, did you?'

Sid gives me one of his funny looks. 'What are you on

about? She merely observed, in the course of ordinary conversation, that she had seen Mr Pomeroy blowing his snitch on a pair of knicks. It was a throwaway piece of information but it made me think. How many men do you know who blow their noses on birds' fleas and ants?'

I shake my head, silent in the presence of a master. 'You've got me there Sid.'

Sid wrinkles up his eyes. 'For a moment I was puzzled, I must confess. And then it came to me: he didn't intend to blow his nose on a pair of knicks!'

'You mean, he was sniffing them?' I say. 'Blimey, that's a bit kinky, isn't it?'

Sid claps a hand to his nut. 'Gordon Bennett! It's going to be agony working with you – he thought the knicks were his handkerchief, don't you see? That's how he gave himself away. He'd obviously had a quick whip round the dormitories and stowed the swag in his jacket pockets.'

'Caught in the knicker time,' I say. 'Blimey, Sid. I have to hand it to you. That was brilliant. I bet your breath came in short pants when you made the final deduction. What a crying shame that fate in the shape of a Sainsbury's trolley should rob you of your finest moment.'

'Lesser men might think like that,' says Sid waving a dismissive mit. 'But I reckon that in this game you've got to be philat-philli—'

'Philosophical?' I prompt.

'That as well,' says Sid 'It's the intellectual satisfaction of having outwitted a master criminal that really makes me chuffed to the bollocks.'

'Very understandably,' I say. 'Tell me, was the butler the geezer who was running round with the knickers over his nut?' Sid shakes his head. 'No, Timmo. That was a red heron. You get a lot of them in this kind of case.'

'Don't you mean a red herring?' I say, thinking once

again that the dicky bird image may not be inapt. Had the Lea nut collided with the floor of the gym, red could indeed have been this year's colour for co-opted love divers.

'As you wish,' says Sid. 'What I'm trying to say is that you get a lot of publicity seekers trying to cash in on the action. The kind of people who confess to murders when they haven't committed them.' Smart readers will observe that my involvement in the whole sorry business has not been discovered. The speed of a naked Lea with a pair of woman's knicks over his nut makes a mockery of Great Britain's lack of success in recent Olympic Hundred Metres finals. 'The bastard who terrorised those poor girls in the gymnasium just wanted a cheap thrill and his name in the papers. It's a good job he got away really. It robbed him of the satisfaction.'

The way I feel after my bout with Titania, Imogen and the rest of them I reckon that I have been robbed of the satisfaction permanently. Percy has about as much verve and devil-may-care vigour as the skin on a mug of cold Horlicks. Every time I pass a bird in the street I can feel him scuttling for shelter.

My rehabilitation is not helped by the unhappy course of my relationship with the fair Gretchen. The tip of my tonk has still to penetrate deeper than the first half inch of her nunga throttler and I am beginning to wonder if I am ever going to feel my cobblers dusting the back of her khyber. Talk about frustrating. It is like trying to play shove halfpenny with your dick. I am thinking of buying percy a Tam O' Shanter and calling him Throb Roy. After every session with Gretchen I am reduced to aching agony. There is nothing worse than having fifteen and a half centimetres of warmobile and finding that the parking space is only big enough for a mini. It is a great pity because at every other level than the horizontal I get on very well with the bird. She is warm and kind and even buys me a present – some Bavarian ornamental mug with a lid on it. I don't reckon it much because it reminds me of the thing Uncle Ted kept spitting in when I visited him in hospital but, of course, I don't let on.

One thing I do find embarrassing is the way that she keeps rabbiting on about my Mum and Dad. She is always asking questions about them and it is clear that she is angling for an invite round to the ancestral seat. I would be chary if she was an English bird but her being German makes the whole idea even more of a liability. I always remember how Dad went spare when he found me having it off with Matilda NGobla. That little bout of in and out pleased him a great deal less than somewhat, and Mum did her nut as well. Of course, Gretchen is not black which is a big step in the right direction as far as any future daughter-in-law is concerned but I am still wary of inviting her to make a mockery of the door mat with 'welcome' written on it.

In the end I decide that to invite her round for a cup of cha can't do any harm and broach the subject with Mum and Dad. 'Be all right if I invite a friend round for tea on Sunday?' I say, dead casual-like.

'Not that boy with the motorbike,' says Mum. 'He left grease marks all over the house.'

'And that was just the stuff that dripped off his bonce,' says Dad. 'Horrible long-haired git! It made my flesh creep to look at him.'

'I wasn't talking about Michel,' I say. 'This is a girl.'

'A girl?' says Mum. The minute she says it I have third thoughts – I have already had second thoughts. 'Oh. That's nice. A friend, is she?' Mum used to treat any bird I got involved with like she had terminal dandruff. Now it is different. I think she is getting worried about me. She keeps talking about Rosie and the kids – Jerome and Jason, or Reggie and Ronny as they are known locally – and saying how most of the neighbourhood tearaways have improved since they 'settled down'. I reckon she would like to see me going up the aisle. 'What's her name?'

'Er – Gretchen,' I say.

'Gretchen?' Dad spits Swiss roll all over the tart in *The Sun* who is demonstrating a new kind of seatbelt in the altogether. 'That's not an English name.'

'That's right,' I say. 'It's German.'

'Blooming stupid!'

Dad gives the bird in *The Sun* a second helping of Swiss roll and spares her further suffering by putting down the paper. 'Fancy giving a little kiddy a Hun name. Some people have got no common.'

'She is German,' I say.

'German?' says Mum, her eyes widening. 'You mean, from Germany?'

'That's right, Mum.' I say. 'Bad Soden.'

'You mind your language in front of your mother!' storms Dad. 'Oh my gawd. I never thought I'd live to see the day. The Nazis marching over my threshold. Achieving by stealth what they could never do in open combat.'

'Come off it, Dad!' I say. 'You're always saying how much you respect the Germans. What hard workers they are, how clean they are and all that.'

'That's as soldiers,' says Dad. 'They're all right to fight against but I don't want them in my home.'

'I don't know what the neighbours will say,' says Mum sounding dead worried.

'They don't have to know, do they?' I say, beginning to get warmed up. 'She's not going to walk down the street carrying a swastika and singing "Deutschland alley lubbers".'

'I wasn't thinking of her coming to tea,' says Mum. 'It's when – well, you know, later on, the banns.'

'I'm putting up a ban right now,' says Dad. 'No son of mine is going to marry a kraut. I didn't fight for six years to keep this country free for my children to grow up in so they could get spliced to the people who were raining fire bombs down on me' – Dad's war effort involved fire watching and building up the largest stock of nicked gas masks in South East England.

'Hang on a minute!' I shout. 'Who said anything about marriage? I'm asking her round for tea, not to choose the wedding cake.'

'I'm not saying we wouldn't like you to settle down,' says Mum. 'To the right girl, of course. I always used to like that girl from Stockwell. What was her name? Tracey Stacey?'

'Lacey,' I say. 'She came from Tooting and you hated her. You were always saying that she wasn't good enough for me.'

'Oh no, dear,' says Mum. 'You're getting confused. I always liked her.'

'At least she wasn't a bleeding kraut,' says Dad. 'Oh dear, you do know how to pick them, don't you?'

'Now listen—!' I say.

'I suppose we'll have to make the best of it,' says Mum. 'You remember that Avril Figgis – the one there was the fight about outside the baths hall – she married a Yank, didn't she?'

'Several from what I heard,' says Dad. 'Darkies, most of them. It near killed her mother, I know that. Her old man resigned from the bowls club.'

'The kiddies weren't black,' says Mum. 'I saw a photo of them in the *Sentinel*.'

'You can never tell what colour anyone is supposed to be

in that rag,' says Dad. 'You remember when Uncle Albert had his presentation down at the British Legion. They made him look like Al Jolson.'

'Ah hem,' I say. 'Do you mind if I interrupt for a minute? Not only am I not getting hitched but I resent all this anti-German rubbish. The war has been over for thirty years, you know. Gretchen belongs to a generation which never knew about all the things the rest of us would have forgotten if it hadn't been for *Colditz* and all those old war movies they show on the telly.'

'They don't change,' says Dad. 'Only their socks, any way. Either at your throat or at your feet. You don't have to tell me nothing about the son honey – I mean, the Hun, sonny.'

'Timmy's right, Walter,' says Mum, her lip quivering like a jelly at a farting contest. 'It's his life. If he wants to marry this girl then there's nothing we can do about it. He's past the age of incontinence. We've done everything we can for him. No mother or father could have done more.' With these touching words she bursts into tears and it takes several minutes of my father comforting her and telling her to belt up before peace is restored.

I continue to try to make it plain that I have no plans to get spliced but I might as well save my breath. With every second that passes, Mum becomes more convinced that her third grandson is going to be called Adolf and it gets so that I am beginning to take the idea seriously myself. Maybe fate is perspiring so that I don't have it off with Gretchen until after we are hitched. Very ironical that would be.

In the end, Mum bends over backwards so far that she ends up saying that Gretchen must come for a proper meal and not just tea. Of course, this is the last thing that I want. The most practical thing that Mum ever did with her *Good Housekeeping Cookery Book* was to use it to prop up one of the wonky legs on the hallstand. Even Attila the Hun and his hungry hordes would have turned their hooters up at the nosh she provides.

Poor unsuspecting Gretchen is delighted to get inside 17 Scraggs Lane at last and even the expression on Dad's face doesn't put her off. 'So nice it is, here, Mr Lea,' she says cheerfully. 'How many interesting things you have. It is like museum. I like old photograph of Kaiser on mantelpiece.'

Dad turns scarlet. 'That's my father!' he says. 'He fought against your Kaiser – or he would have if he hadn't taken the wrong tram on the way to join up and lost his memory. It was a terrible experience for him. He never forgot it.'

'And all these old umbrellas,' continues Gretchen, quite relaxed. 'I know it rain a lot in England but why you have them?'

'They always come in handy,' says Dad, obviously loth to admit that he nicks everything he can lay his hands on down at the Lost Property Office where he spends most of his waking hours – and quite a few of the ones when he is having a crafty kip.

'Hello dear,' says Mum coming in and wiping her hands on her apron. 'I hope father hasn't been having a go at you because of what happened during the war. It's all over now and I say let bygones be bygones. I'm certain there was good and bad on both sides and if what Mrs Coles says about her husband is anything to go by then we've nothing to be proud of. She's a nice woman but you can never get away from her. You know what I mean? I often think—'

'Mum! Please!' I hiss. Honestly, my Mum and Dad do so little entertaining that when anyone comes, Mum gets an attack of the verbal squitters. Nobody else can get a word in. It would be all right if anybody had ever met any of the people she rabbits on about or even if she finished one story before she went on to the next but she gets carried away.

'Your husband has been showing me his treasures,' says Gretchen. 'So unusual, the idea of the stuffed birds on the furniture.'

I think it is bloody stupid myself. Especially with all the stains there are about. The birds just draw attention to them. Dad gets some really stupid thoughts wedged between his bottles sometimes. I hate stuffed birds at the best of times and it is decidely diabolical when you settle back in a chair and a blackheaded gull pecks you in the earhole.

'I have prepared a special German meal for you,' says Mum, striking fresh terror into my heart. 'Worst liver.'

At first I think she means liverwurst, but not after I have tasted it. Honestly, if you could get your soles repaired with that stuff you would put every shoemaker in the country out of business. I see Gretchen wince when she takes the first mouthful and as for the sauerkraut, that is unbelievable. It tastes like red tea leaves. By the time we get to the Black Forest Cherry Cake I am ready to throw in the sponge. Mum has quite clearly thrown in the sponge, not to mention the remains of a Dundee cake, half a slab of Battenburg and a packet of wafers. Talk about awful. A few more meals like that and Mum could be in line for *Lives of the Great Poisoners*.

What amazes me is that Gretchen manages to nosh everything that is put in front of her. It is a performance of real character and it makes me wonder what the food at her hotel must be like. I make the excuse that she has to be back early because she is on duty, and drag her away as soon as Mum has made a pot of tea. 'Why you do that?' she says. 'I was enjoying evening.'

'I was thinking about a way you might enjoy it a lot more,' I say, thrusting her back into a convenient doorway and making immediate contact with her cakehole. 'Oh Gretchen, I do want to make love to you.' Just to make sure that she understands what I am talking about, I dart my hand under her coat and spread my mit over her grumble. I can feel her swelling like a silk pin cushion and I wish I could slot a couple of digits and follow up with the star attraction. Percy is probing north by north west and Gretchen presses her hand against him and sucks in breath.

'I want, too,' she says.

I know it is dead dicey to mess about in shop doorways but I am getting carried away and I want something to show for the evening. Just a feel would be better than nothing. When you have got something like six inches of burnished steel going for you it deserves exposure to the risk of a spot of appreciation. We are necking in the entrance to a large shoe shop so I pull her round the corner into one of the glass lay-bys with a view of ten inch platform heels and whip open my fly. Perce leaps to the hand and I guide one of her appropriately named Germans to my love object.

'Do something,' I say. 'I can't go on like this.' There is a strained edge to my voice and although she might produce a bow and play 'Way down upon the Swannee River' on my tonk, I rather hope that she will realise that relief lies in a different quarter.

'It's hot,' she whispers. She sounds fascinated and I press myself against her and move up and down on the balls of my feet. I am so worked up that I am practically coming.

'What do you think you're doing?' The tone of voice suggests that the speaker has a very clear idea of what we are doing. Gretchen freezes and withdraws her hand immediately. The handbag she has round her wrist slips and falls towards the floor. Eager not to share the secret of my impulsive nature with the fuzz – for it is indeed one of their ilk who has slunk round the corner on a thrill quest – I turn away from full frontal exposure and move deeper into the recesses of the shop to repair the damage. I do not drop my mits to my rampant rogerer as this will immediately give the game away to anyone standing behind me. It is something of a surprise to me to find that the innermost sector of the display area has been occupied by a gentleman of the road. He is lying back against a window full of 'Spring's exciting colours!' under a blanket of newspapers and his eyes are just beginning to flicker shut as I make my appearance. They open pretty wide when they clock a gander at me and his bonce clonks back against the glass.

'Do me a favour, son,' he says. 'If you're going to carry a handbag, don't hang it on your prick!'

# CHAPTER EIGHT

In which Timmy and Sid set out to meet a contact in a Turkish bath and Timmy measures his length with sun- and fun-loving Nadia Durrant in the Solarium. An encounter which has unexpected consequences.

'I had a bloke round the office today,' says Sid, all excited.

'Makes a change from the cleaners,' I say.

'Shut up,' says Sid. 'You know what I mean. A client – well, I think he was a client.'

'We could do with some of those,' I say. 'That second leaflet drop in the Co-op didn't pay dividends, did it?'

'It should have done,' says Sid. 'You expect to get a divi at the Co-op, don't you?'

'Very whimsical,' I say. 'Tell me more about this bloke.'

'He was funny,' says Sid. 'Didn't give anything away. He seemed dead relieved when I told him I hadn't been to a public school.'

'Public school?' I say. 'You must have been having a very funny conversation.'

'That's what I said,' says Sid. 'Very strange it was. He wanted to know if we'd ever been to Russia.'

'Blooming nearly,' I say, thinking back to the time when Sid cast me adrift in the Thames and I was picked up by a Russian freighter – see *Confessions of a Long-Distance Lorry Driver* for thrill-packed details.

'I didn't mention that,' says Sid. 'Some sixth sense – call it intuition if you like – or perhaps my carefully developed powers of deduction—'

'Get on with it,' I say.

'Suggested that he didn't want us to have been to Russia.

Anyway, I've got the gen and we've got to go and see his guv'nor.'

'Great,' I say. 'Where does he hang out?'

'That's another funny thing,' says Sid. 'We've got to go to a Turkish bath where we'll be picked up.'

'I bet we will,' I say. 'I've heard all about that. You never want to lie down in one of those cubicles, you know.'

'Picked up by a contact who will take us to our man,' says Sid through gritted teeth.

'Not General Arman?' I say. 'The fat black bloke who wants to marry the Queen. I don't fancy working for him. He's vicious.'

'That's General Amin, you berk!' says Sid. 'Gordon Bennett! You have absolutely no contraception about what's going on in the world, do you?'

'I'm sorry, Sid,' I say. 'How do we know which is the right bloke?'

'Well, he's Jewish for a start-off,' says Sid. 'I can't remember the name. The geezer wouldn't let me write anything down.'

'Brilliant,' I say. 'So I keep my eyes open for a hampton with a short back and sides. That could be anybody. You don't have to be a four by two to be skinned alive.'

'That's not the only thing,' says Sid. 'He'll be wearing a tattoo. A red dragon.'

'Where?' I say.

'Down at the Turkish baths,' says Sid. 'Don't you ever listen to anything?'

'I meant where on his body?' I say. 'On his flowers and frolics? His fife and drum? His Marquis of Lorne?'

'I don't know,' says Sid. 'It can't be very difficult to spot a red dragon, can it?'

But it is very difficult. Those Turkish baths are dead steamy and the wooden slatted seats don't help. I have just tapped a bloke on the shoulder and pointed to his bum when I see that what I thought was a red dragon, is in fact the mark left by the bench he was sitting on. Talk about embarrassing. As I have already indicated, you can make some very funny friends like that. This bloke is impossible to shake off and I am making a dash for the dry heat room when Sid looms up.

'Excellent,' he says, getting it all wrong as usual. 'You've found our man.'

'*Our* man?' squeaks my new chum. 'Oooh, lovely!'

'Where do you want us to go?' says Sid.

'Well, I don't mind,' twitters the poufdah. 'Your place, my place, it's all the same to me. A change is as good as a rest isn't it?'

'Is that a password?' says Sid. 'They didn't tell me anything about passwords.'

More like arseword, I think to myself, suppressing a shudder. 'Er – Sid,' I say, trying to make signs to him without Cedric seeing. 'This isn't our man.'

'Oh no,' says Sid, looking down. 'His dick's not right, is it?'

'Oh, it's like that, is it?' says the ginger drawing himself up to his full five foot seven and a half inches. 'Hoity toity, are we? Blowing hot and cold – ooh! the very thought of it – just playing with me, were you? Right, we'll see about that! Julian! Tristram!'

'What the—?' Before Sid can sort out his uncertainty a couple of muscular pooves appear wearing earrings and petulant expressions. 'What's up – I hope – Jerry-baby?' says one of them.

'We've got some funny boys here who are looking for a stinging slap on the wrist,' says Jerry-baby. 'They've just trampled all over my susceptibilities.'

'I never touched his sus-suss-whatsits!' says Sid. 'You

belt up or I'll shove your hampton through your mate's earring!'

It is at this point that what Mum calls 'unpleasantness' begins to break out. Sid can be very punchy when faced with someone half his size and has never been partial to tickles (Tickle your fancy: nancy. Ed.). Strong words are bandied about and I deem it best to step back into the clouds of steam that make the scene of the argument look like a pantomime stage just after the demon king has appeared. Sid is more than capable of looking after himself and I am not prone to aggro – by it, sometimes, but not to it.

The atmosphere is getting on my wick so I wrap my towel round my waist and let myself out into the corridor that leads back to the changing room. I have taken half a dozen paces when I come to a door marked 'Solarium'. I wonder what happens in there? No harm in finding out. I open the door and find myself looking at what appears to be a large X-ray machine. There is a mass of apparatus set in the ceiling and a couch-like structure beneath. Stretched out on the couch is a beautifully tanned bint wearing two pads over her mince pies and pink varnish on her toe nails – nothing else. She does not move her head as I come in but sighs loudly.

'I suppose you want to share,' she says. She starts to move over and I watch the firm honey-coloured flesh ripple. One of her knockers flops from right to left and I bite my lip. 'Come on.' She pats the couch beside her and I am on to it like a cat on to Dad's favourite armchair. I have read about this kind of thing – I mean, artificial sunshine and all that. You have to be careful of your eyes but otherwise it is just like the real thing. I wrap my towel into a pad, place it over my minces and settle down beside Miss Delectable. Of course it leaves my dick exposed but it has survived in hotter places. A touch of dark brown magic might lend lustre to my cluster: 'and now, from darkest Clapham, Timothy Lea and his congo bongo . . .' I stretch out my toes and feel the warmth soaking into every pore of my body. This is the life. Much better than having a wrist slapping match with a gang of gingers. You can stuff that for a lark. I allow a sigh of ecstasy to escape from my lips and win an immediate response from my partner.

'Heaven isn't it?' she breathes. 'It reminds me of Rimini.'

'Uhm,' I say. I was thinking of Southend with the tide out, myself. It is amazing how sun worship and all that kick makes people forget their hang-ups. This bird is lying there perfectly relaxed and she doesn't know me from Adam – especially in my present condition. If I sat next to her in the bus she would probably change seats. Maybe the world would be a better place if we went around starkers all the time. Nobody would be able to dress flash and make out they were better than anyone else. Still I suppose the blokes with the big dicks would reckon that they were better than the blokes with the little dicks and the blokes with the little dicks would be jealous of the blokes with the big dicks. Whatever happened they would have it in for each other – given half a chance.

I am lying there exercising my mind with this kind of stimulating thought when the bird brushes her arm against mine.

'Sorry,' she murmurs. 'Um, you're very muscular, aren't you?'

'I try to keep myself in shape,' I say.

'AARH! !' I nearly jump out of my foreskin because the bird grabs hold of my dick and levers herself to an upright position.

She chucks my love truncheon aside like it has given her

an electric shock and looks down at me, mincepies blazing. 'You've got an infernal cheek!' she accuses. 'It's women only from twelve o'clock. Are you trying to be funny?'

'I may never smile again, lady,' I say gazing down at my crumpled horn and realising how a tube strap must feel. 'I'm sorry but I'm a stranger here. When you told me to hop aboard I thought it must be all right.'

The lady looks slightly chastened and feels for one of her eye pads. The other one has landed just above my Mad Mick so, when she hesitates, I hand it back to her. Little gestures like that mean a lot to a woman. 'I can see that it wasn't all your fault,' she says. 'I'm sorry I – I—'

'That's all right,' I say. 'No hard feelings.' I don't mean to be funny but we both have a little laugh and I know that the ice has been broken – maybe not just the ice. Only time will tell.

'Nadia Durrant,' she says leaning back beside me and pausing for a moment before replacing her eyepads with a shrug. 'A strange place to bump into someone.'

'Timothy Lea,' I say. 'Yes, still, it's very nice here, isn't it?'

'Lovely,' she says. 'Have you got the time?'

'It must be about one,' I say. 'Hang on a minute – I don't mean that literally, of course. I couldn't stand the experience twice in one day.' We have another little laugh at my scintillating sense of humour and I bend over the side of the bed to look at my watch. As I do so, my foot digs into the soft flesh of her calf and I hear her wince. 'I'm sorry,' I say. 'We seem to be handing out a lot of punishment to each other. It's five past one.'

'That means I'm done on this side,' says the bird, starting to turn over.

'Uhm,' I say, checking the first words that spring to my lips. 'How long do you give it?'

Nadia stretches her arms out beside her and turns her head towards me so that it is resting on the pillow. Her eyes flicker lazily. 'It gets a bit longer every time,' she says. 'You build up.'

It may be my imagination but I think that her fingers are brushing against the side of my thigh. I let one of my hands stray towards them and pull the towel back over my eyes.

'How long do you think I ought to give it?' I say.

'It depends on your skin,' says Nadia. 'You're quite dark, aren't you?' It is not my imagination. The bint is definitely touching me up. It is subtle but unmistakable. Percy is beginning to twitch even before her naughty pandy brushes against my knob.

'Quite dark,' I say. 'I don't burn easily.' I begin to dust her back bumpers gently with my fingertips and she burrows into the couch and wrinkles her nose. Her own looks and lingers are now checking that fast growing percy is operational. This could be the start of something beautiful. I know I should be thinking about the kangaroo with the dragon tattooed on his how's your father but I can't seem to get motivated somehow – that's a good word, isn't it? The bag of coke down the Labour was always using it. He said I was dead Gert and Daisy (lazy. Ed) and had no motivation.

'This is ridiculous,' says Nadia. For a moment I think she is talking about my hampton and the news does not chuff me overmuch. Then I realise that she is going through the standard female bit of facing up to reality, remembering where we are, not being a stupid fool etc, etc. It is not going to change anything. It is just a manoeuvre that some birds have to go through before they have it off. The same way that a dog turns round a couple of times before it sits down.

'No it isn't,' I say. That may not seem like the greatest reassurance you have ever heard but it will do. Most of the time, birds are not listening to what you say anyway. They just want to hear a voice filling the gaps when they stop rabbiting to draw breath, pictures on the nursery wall, or the old age pension – it depends what age they are. That old Joey (Maxim. Ed.) about actions speaking louder than words was never truer than when applied to mothers of pearl. Chat is very nice if you have got it but 'get 'em orf, gal!' delivered with the right edge to the voice works just as well. I had a mate called Reg Dicker when I was at Ponty (Pontypool: school. Ed.) He was so dumb that he had to ask the bloke next to him what to say when we had roll call. He could get a bird's knicks off just by the way he looked at her. Most of the judies who went out with him did not even bother to wear them. Once he gave them the old Dicker slow burn they began to curl at the edges. I was dead grateful when his family moved down to Dartmoor because they wanted to be near his old man.

Nadia Durrant has temporarily stopped remodelling my hampton while she enjoys her burst of conscience but now she starts again and I sink my digits into the inviting cleft between her back bumpers. She open her legs to make it easier for me and I slide my hand down until it brushes against a few silky lair hairs and makes contact with the lower end of juice junction. The moment I touch her fun box she lets out a long sigh and tightens her grip on my Mad Mick like she is frightened it might make a bolt for it. Percy is now in what you might call an exposed state and it occurs to me that all the ultra violet may have an ultra violent effect on my old friend. Best to tuck him away somewhere nice and dark. Any suggestions? What a good idea! I would never have thought of that in a month of oozedays. Rising swiftly to my knees, I find Nadia flipping over on to her back and clearly eager for action.

'Kiss me there!' she pants, straining her arms down her body. It is clear that the lady is desirous of a grumble mumble and, never one to disappoint, I spread apart her luscious bridges (Bridge of Sighs: thighs. Ed) and prepare to dive. But hist! What have we here? There, clearly tattooed a few inches from her snatch, is a small red dragon! This puts a completely different complexion on it, as the actress said to the Nigerian bishop in a similar position to myself. Professional ethics demand that I immediately find Sid and tell him that I have made cuntact with our contact – I mean, well, you know what I mean.

'Go on!' breathes Nadia. 'Do it to me, please!'

It is difficult, isn't it? What would you do in a situation like that? Yes, me too. Sid can wait ten minutes. Maybe twenty. After all, he is always rabbiting on about the importance of hard work and this is an occasion when I can really get my head down.

# CHAPTER NINE

In which Timmy and Sid are recruited by P to become C Men for Mission E – known as Emission in some circles. Also in in which Felicity and Miss Diver check out our heroes' Resistence Quotient.

When Sid comes upon me – I used the expression wishing I hadn't – I am standing outside the Solarium in a state of considerable pain and exhaustion.

'There you are!' says Sid. 'Where the hell have you been?'

'Ooh Sid,' I say. 'I haven't half got a sore bum!'

Sid looks dead worried. 'Those bleeding poufs didn't get you, did they?' he says. 'You haven't been nobbled?'

'Nobbled, nibbled, everything,' I say. 'No Sid, it's the sunray lamp in that place. My back's been roasted.' It is a fact, too. By the time I got off Nadia my Cilla (Cilla Black: back. Ed.) has been exposed to more ultra violet rays than you get in half a lifetime's holidays at Cleethorpes. I can hardly bear to feel anything against it. The towel round my fife is agony.

'Solarium,' says Sid, looking at the door. 'Blimey, I think this is it!'

'What are you on about?' I say.

'What that bloke said to me!' says Sid getting all excited. 'It wasn't a Jewish geezer it was that place! Don't you see, I thought he was talking about somebody called Sol Arium but he was talking about a solarium.'

'Brilliant,' I say.

Of course, I am being dead sarcastical but Sid does not see that. 'Thanks,' he says. 'It's just reasoning ability, really. Either you've got it or you haven't. You, for instance. You could spend half an hour in that place and never come across anything.'

'Highly unlikely,' I say, thinking of the way Nadia spun-dried my action man kit.

'Let's get in there,' says Sid. 'Blimey, without me you'd be lost, wouldn't you?'

I don't say anything but let him crash through the door.

Nadia is just pulling on her knicks and she looks up angrily.

'I'm sorry,' says Sid. 'I was – er looking for the – er—'

'It's down the end of the corridor on the right,' snaps Nadia. 'Now stop gawping and get out of here!'

'Er – the red dragon,' stammers Sid.

Nadia pulls down her knicks and gives Sid a flash that reveals all. 'Come inside and close the door,' she says. 'What kept you so long? I was getting bored waiting.'

'That's right,' I say. She was, wasn't she?

'Were you in on this?' says Sid.

'In a manner of speaking – yes,' I say. 'I got on to Miss Durrant half an hour ago.'

'It's not Miss Durrant,' says the bird. 'That's just a pseudonym. You can call me Friday.'

'Great,' says Sid. 'What do you fancy doing? A few pints of apple fritter down the rubber?'

'She's talking about her code name, Sid!' I explain. Honestly, he takes so long to catch on that I get worried sometimes.

'Come on!' says Friday, tucking her knockers away into her bra with a gesture that makes percy perk up. 'We must go to P.'

'Funny you should say that,' says Sid. 'I was just feeling like a gypsy's kiss.'

'She's not talking about a Jimmy Riddle!' I say.

'Exactly,' says Friday. 'P is our leader. I will take you to him.'

'What's all this about?' says Sid. 'Why does P want to see us?'

Friday shakes her head. 'You will have to ask him that yourself,' she says. 'It is more than my life is worth to reveal anything to you.'

I would have thought different myself, but I don't say anything and half an hour later we are in the reception area of a large block of flats somewhere in the Fulham area. There are three lifts in front of us, one of them with an out of order notice on it.

'Is this where P hangs out?' I say. 'I expected something more secret after all that palava about picking us up at the Turkish baths.'

'Ah,' says the shapely Friday. 'When you get in the lift you will find that everything is not what it appears to be.'

'Say no more,' says Sid, tapping his hooter knowingly. 'I've got it. This is going to amaze you.' So saying, he opens the lift door with the out of order sign on it and falls ten feet into a pool of oil at the bottom of the lift shaft. Fortunately, he lands on his nut so no serious damage is done.

'What made you do that?' I say when we have fished him out.

'I thought the out of order sign was to conceal the existence of a special lift that took you to a floor not serviced by the other lifts. It was just a hunch.'

'You want to watch those hunches,' I say. 'They could be fatal. I can see the subscription for your gravestone—'

'You mean the *in*scription *on* my gravestone,' says Sid.

'I can see that as well,' I say. ' "Gone to hunch".'

'Come on,' says Friday. 'We are late and P does not like to be kept waiting.'

'I know how he feels,' says Sid. 'I don't like being kept waiting for a P either.'

Friday and I exchange sympathetic glances and I sense that she is grateful to know that there is someone around with my comparative suavity and innate good breeding. We go into another lift and Sidney eventually stops yukking at his terrible joke.

'Right,' says Friday. 'You are now at the threshold of Mission E.'

'Emission,' says Sid. 'Blimey! I've heard of that.'

'You practically invented it,' I say. 'What I—' Before I can say anything else, Friday pushes one of the buttons on the panel and we hear the sound of a door opening. Sid who has been looking towards me, steps forward and flattens his boat race against the lift doors which are still shut. It is the back of the lift that has opened. A narrow corridor goes off at right angles to the lift and it is clear that we have been cunningly conveyed into the building next to the one we entered.

'Help your friend and follow me,' says Friday.

I lead Sid, who has his hand wedged over his hooter, down the corridor and we come to another lift. It is much smaller than the first one and it is a squeeze for us all to get in it. I have already been pressed up against Friday so I give Sid a go. I am busy trying to keep my roasted back away from the wall, Friday is trying to keep away from Sid's grease-stained suiting and all in all, it can't be the most comfortable journey any of us have ever made. We practically fall in to the corridor when the door slides open.

The decor is a lot different to what it was at the bottom of the lift. Bright lights and thick carpets compared to shabby lino. Friday moves swiftly down another corridor and we follow her into what turns out to be an outer office occupied by a red-headed bird carrying her knockers like she ... ggle cannon balls. She gives Sid and me what you might describe as a cool, level look.

'Hello, Jenny,' says Friday. 'I'm delivering the merchandise. I'm sorry I'm so late but there was a cock-up at the Solarium.'

'I know there was,' says Jenny disapprovingly. 'We saw it going up on close circuit television.' She nods towards a screen set in the wall, and Friday blushes. 'Come this way, er – gentlemen. P is expecting you.'

'So much for the secret service,' sighs Friday.

'Goodbye Friday,' I say. 'Thanks for showing us the way.'

'You showed me the way too, darling,' coos my erstwhile belt seductively. 'It was lovely. Let's hope we get to meet on an assignment.'

'Did you have it off with her?' says Sid as we are shown into the main office. 'You crafty sod! All I got was half a dozen poufs flicking my bum with wet towels.'

'At least they had a whip round for you,' I say.

The room we have been shown into is heavy with wood panelling except on a wall that is completely covered in books. In front of the window is a large desk with a globe standing on it. Behind the desk is a distinguished looking geezer with silver hair brushed back from his forehead – he would look bloody stupid if it was brushed forward, wouldn't he? – and at his elbow a thick-set bloke wearing his hair in the Kojak fashion – that is, somewhere where it is not connected to his head. They seem to be saying goodbye to someone because, in front of them, a bloke in frogman suit, oxygen cylinder and flippers rips off a racy salute and bounds towards what we soon see is a private bathroom. He leaps on to the toilet pedestal, tears off another salute, and drops into the lavatory bowl pulling the chain as he goes. There is a familiar noise and he disappears from sight.

Silver Bonce turns to us with a catch in his voice. 'There goes one of our best agents,' he says.

'He was certainly flushed with success,' says Sid.

'Probably effluent in several languages,' I chip in.

An expression akin to pain ruckles Silver Bonce's features but he shrugs it off and extends a hand towards Sid. 'P,' he says.

'No thanks,' says Sid. 'I've just—' Fortunately, I manage to stamp on his foot before he can say anything else and he starts to hop round the room screeching and cursing.

'Timothy Lea,' I say. 'I'm sorry we're late. It's quite difficult to get here, isn't it?'

'Especially if you've come from an oil rig,' says P looking at Sidney with a puzzled expression on his mug. 'Is that where your associate learned his highland dancing? I've always wondered what you did in the evenings.'

'Pull yourself together, Sid,' I say. 'The gentleman's talking to us.'

Sid cools down and P waves us towards a couple of chairs. It is a bit unfortunate that we both decide to sit in the same one but, then these things always happen when you're trying to make a good impression – like the way you always piss over your boots when you've put on a new pair of suedes.

'I expect you're wondering what this is all about?' says P.

'If it's anything to do with our tax returns when we were cleaning windows, then that was the time when I had all the trouble with my memory,' says Sid. 'My brother-in-law here will vouch—'

'No,' says P. 'We're nothing to do with the tax people.

This is Mission E. E for emergency. Britain's last line of defence against those many perils that now threaten our island home. The super elite of the British Intelligence Service.'

'Blimey,' says Sid. 'Well, you don't have to worry about us. We've always been very patriotic. I've still got my World Cup Willy. And we'd have murdered those bleeding Krauts if we'd been allowed to play them in the last final. Those fluid ball skills of the Dutch fellers were all very well but what your Kraut needs is Norman Hunter tattooing his ankles.'

'I don't know what you're talking about but your patriotism has never been exposed to scrutiny,' says P.

'I'm glad to hear it,' says Sid.

'I've had you brought here because, to the best of our knowledge, you're the only organisation of your type in this country that hasn't been infiltrated by the Ruskies. Isn't that so, Boris?'

P turns to the menacing-looking geezer by his side who nods like one of those Alsatians lunatics have in the back windows of their cars. 'That is indeed true, Comrade Chief.'

He smiles to himself and wanders across the room, humming 'The Vulgar Boatman' or some such melody with a lot of 'Yo-o heave ho's!' in it. I can't put my finger on it but there is something about him that makes me feel uneasy.

P turns to Sid. 'To the best of your knowledge you've never been infiltrated have you?'

Sid looks uncomfortable. 'I came bloody close this afternoon,' he says. 'I don't reckon that Turkish bath as a pick-up joint, it's more like a prick-up joint. Know what I mean? All right if you want to enlarge the circle of your friends but I wouldn't bend over to pick up a box of matches.'

'I think you'll find we're free from taint,' I say hurriedly. 'What exactly did you have in mind for us – er, Mr. P?'

'Not so fast, young man,' says P, leaning across his desk and fixing me with a steely eye that seems to dig into me like one of those knives that horses use to get boy scouts out of their hooves. 'There are more questions to be asked before you become one of our happy band.'

'Not Nat Temple's lot,' says Sid. 'I used to like them. Always good for a giggle.'

P finds it easy to ignore Sid and his voice grows even more serious. 'Have either of you ever been members of the Communist Party or plotted to overthrow the government of this country – even when you were at nursery school?'

'No,' I gulp.

'No,' says Sid.

'Promise?' We nod our agreement. 'Good, then that's settled. I'm sorry I had to ask you that question but we can't afford to take any chances.'

'That's all right,' I say. 'We quite understand. When the security of our country is at stake you can't be too careful.'

'I'm glad you—' P breaks off our conversation and shouts across the room to Boris who appears to be photographing a folder full of papers marked 'Jolly Secret' with a tiny camera that looks more like a cigarette lighter. 'Boris! Don't bother to do that. How many times do I have to tell you? Records put everything on microfilm.'

'Smileski.' P smiles obediently and Boris clicks off another shot before putting away the camera in the breast pocket of his smock. 'Sorry, Comrade Chief. I forget. I always think it best to have two copies of everything to be on safe side.'

P shakes his head in admiration. 'Damn efficient chap,

that. The country could do with more like him.' Boris smiles modestly and P turns back to us. 'One more very important thing. Are either of you homosexuals?' I shake my head firmly and Sid does the same. 'Damn!' says P. 'Still, you can't have everything. You don't get a Burgess and Maclean every day of the week.'

'Too true, Squire,' says Sid who clearly has no idea what the gentleman is talking about – dental hygiene never being his strong point.

'Right,' says P. 'Now we have dispensed with the formalities, I can start filling you in.'

'You fancy your chances a bit, don't you?' says Sid.

'Dicing with death, I'd call it. I'd only have to give you my old one-two, followed by my three-four and you'd be getting your head down without any of the fringe benefits.'

'Sid!' I say. 'Pull yourself together. Surely it's obvious that the gentleman wishes to discuss the possibility of us undertaking an assignment.'

'There's no possibility involved,' says P with a new cold edge to the voice. 'You're now C men and there's only one way you can be discharged.'

'C Men?' I say.

'Combat Men,' snaps P. 'Combat Men for Mission Emergency. The highest calling a British man or woman can aspire to. You only sever your connection with the service upon death.'

'What about my old age pension?' says Sid. 'If I'm not allowed to retire, I'll never to able to get it, will I?'

'Old age will be one of the least of your problems,' says P.

'What you're trying to say is that we're in whether we like it or not,' I say. 'There's no turning back.'

'Right,' says P. 'C Men never turn back. If you hadn't

agreed to my terms I would have had no alternative but to liquidate you.'

'You dirty old sod,' says Sid. 'I thought the chalk stripe in your suit was a bit wide. You're a raving poufdah, aren't you? I can't get away from them. Come on Timmo, let's get back to the gutter where we belong.'

'Not so fast, Mr. Noggett.' Sid has only taken one step towards the door when P's hand darts to a button at the side of his desk and there is a sound like a refrigerator switching itself on. Sid's arms claw the air but his feet remain rooted to the carpet. It is as if they have been paralysed or – yes! A powerful magnet must be restraining him via the nails in the bottom of his shoes. What a diabolically complicated and expensive idea. No wonder we pay so much income tax.

'Boris, make sure that Mr. Noggett does not go anywhere in a hurry.' P's voice is as cold as a snowman's arsehole and my blood freezes when I see Boris produce a wicked looking flick knife from his Lucy Locket and take a step towards my unfortunate brother-in-law. Could this be the unkindest cut of all? Yes! As I close my eyes in horror I hear the telltale snipping noise and Sid's pitiful cry of distress – Boris has cut through his braces.

The current is switched off and Sid hobbles towards P's desk with his hands deep in his trouser pockets. 'Right,' says P. 'Now that we know where we all stand, let's get down to business. First of all I'm going to show you some photographs.'

Sid whips out a hand and his trousers fall down. Oh dear.

I know that if I were teamed up with Roger Moore, none of this would be happening. I must ring his agent when I get back to the office. Sid bends down, cracking his nut on the side of the desk, and I take a gander at the photos.

Blimey! Or, to be more specific – phew! I have never seen anything like it.

'I can see that you're disgusted,' says P.

'Oh yes,' I say, hoping that percy is not appearing above desk level. 'They're a bit near the knuckle, aren't they?' In fact, they are nowhere near the knuckle. They are near a lot of other places of a far more intimate nature. Places that don't usually arrive at the cakehole with quite the force and frequency of knuckles.

'Let's have a look,' says Sid. 'Blimey!' He snatches at one of the photographs and his trousers fall down again.

'You might as well leave them there,' says P. 'I'll have the carpet shampooed when you've left.'

'These photographs!' gasps Sid. 'They're all of famous people. I mean, that's the Prime Minister! – I wonder how he manages to do that with his pipe in his mouth. And that bird hanging from the chandelier. That's – ooh, what's her name? It's on the tip of my tongue.'

'It's on the tip of her tongue and all,' I say. 'Amazing, I never knew Jerry Thorpe was like that.'

'He isn't,' says P. 'That's skilful retouching.'

'It is when you're balancing on a one-wheel bicycle,' says Sid. 'I have to give him that.'

'What I'm trying to say is that they're forgeries,' says P. 'None of those pillars of the establishment actually took part in those disgusting acts of group depravity.'

'Not even Tony Booth?' says Sid. 'Surely, he must have done.'

'No,' says P. 'Not even him. We're up against a master craftsman.'

'Just like the bird in this one,' says Sid. 'You'd never think you could get it from that angle, would you?'

'It's easier when you rest your feet on the suit of armour,' I say.

'Silence!' shouts P. 'You don't seem to realise how serious this is. At the moment, these skilful forgeries – the faces of well known people retouched on to photographs of orgies – are appearing all over the country. Somebody is trying to subvert the democratic procedure.'

'I don't get it,' I say.

'You would if you were standing where Margaret Thatcher is in this one,' says Sid. 'Ted Heath's—'

'Shut up!' yells P.

'All over the deck,' says Sid as P rips the photographs from his hand.

'What somebody is trying to do is to make a mockery of British institutions and the august personages who invest them with the dignity and sense of purpose that makes them the envy of nations throughout the world. Once we lose respect for those who govern us we are doomed! The doors of the Augean stables will be thrown open wide and it will be impossible for the rule of law and order to prevail.' He snatches one of the photographs from the pile. 'How could you ever take Harold Wilson seriously again when you had seen him running stark naked behind Barabara Castle with his meerschaum in one hand and a tickle stick in the other?'

Sid nods. 'You're right. I don't think I will ever feel the same way about him. It's diabolical, isn't it? You wouldn't be able to watch a party political broadcast again, would you? – mind you, I find it pretty difficult at the moment.'

'They're no respecters of persons, are they?' I say, pointing to the photograph now on the top of the pile.

'They've even got you there – with the six choirboys – that's very unpleasant, isn't it?'

'Give me that!' P snatches the photo and stuffs it inside his jacket. 'I don't know how that got there. You can forget about that one.'

'I'd be glad to,' says Sir. 'Tell me, P, have you got any idea who's behind this?'

'None,' says P. 'We've reached a dead end. That's why Boris here suggested that we brought you in. He said that we needed some new blood.'

Boris nods and smiles. 'New blood. Oh yesk. Ho ho.'

'Of course the Ruskies are at the bottom of it, you need have no fears about that,' says P. 'The Reds are everywhere.'

Boris nods and gives another of his strange smiles. I wish I knew what it was about that man. It is certainly not his after shave lotion. He smells like a ferrets' fall out shelter.

'Do the police know about this?' I say.

'They are pursuing their own investigations. There is no question of collaboration. When you leave this building you will be on your own.'

'What support will we get?' asks Sid.

'None. The secrecy of this mission demands that we will have to disown you publicly if your cover is blown.'

'Great,' says Sid. 'Do we get luncheon vouchers?'

'You will be taken care of,' says P. 'Yes, Boris?'

'Oh yes,' says Boris. 'They will be taken care of. Have no fear of that.' He starts laughing again and I wonder why he has USSR embroidered on his smock. It must stand for something and it can't be his initials. Underwater Stoat Stranglers Reunion? It doesn't seem very likely.

'I'll hand you over to Miss Diver. She'll show you the rest of the photographs. Some of them feature dogs and that might give you a lead.' P stands up and pounds a fist against the palm of his hand. 'At all costs these swine must be apprehended. It's up to you. Good luck and remember, if there's anything you need, don't bother to ask for it because you won't get it.'

The door closes behind us and Miss Diver wrinkles her nostrils like a whiff of Canal No 5 has attempted to force its way up her delicate hooter. 'Come this way,' she says coldly. 'I'll take you to the debriefing room.'

Sid is obviously excited by this news because he steps forward briskly and collapses on his face when his trousers fall down again. What a prize nana he looks! I watch him shuffling down the corridor, covered in grease from the lift shaft, his boat race a mass of bumps and bruises and try and prevent my heart sinking into my daisies. How can this man save Britain in her darkest hour? He doesn't look as if he could lug a sack of coal up your front steps without tipping half of it into the basement.

'Here we are.' Miss Diver's brisk, efficient voice jerks me back to the present. We are in a thickly carpeted room dotted with comfortable armchairs. 'Take a seat.'

'Ta,' says Sid. 'Nice place you've got here. You don't have a bit of string on you, do you?'

Miss Diver is wrestling with the door of a metal cupboard and she ignores Sid's question.

'Can I—?' I begin but Sid pushes me aside and grabs hold of the offending handle.

'Allow me,' he says. 'I am perfectly equipped to deal with this situation. Muscular dexterity allied to a physical strength that is almost terrifying in its controlled simplicity.'

So saying, he wrenches open the door, and a body and a lot of photographs fall out. Sid's trousers fall down as he catches the corpse and for a few moments they stagger round the room as if competing in a dance marathon. I almost expect to hear Victor Sylvester in the background. Sid is gibbering with terror, which is not surprising, and I have got the mockers up me something horrible, but Miss Diver remains very much in control of her emotions.

'Damn!' she says. 'I do wish people would file things in the right places. Over here.' She opens another cupboard door and I look down to see a shaft like a coal chute running off at an angle. 'Pop him down here.'

'But—'

'Come on!' Miss Diver plucks at the corpse's sleeve and, with Sid's help, drags it to the cupboard before giving it a final push into the yawning darkness. There is a few seconds' pause and then the faint but unmistakable sound of a heavy object making contact with water. 'Right!' says Miss Diver dusting her hands together. 'To business.'

'Who was that?' gasps Sid.

'The last man that P interviewed for a job with the Mission,' says Jenny Diver. 'We found out that he had been buying Polish bacon at Sainsburys.'

'The swine,' says Sid. 'It just shows you can never tell about people, doesn't it?'

Miss Diver does not reply but drops to her hands and knees and starts picking up photographs and a variety of masks, false moustaches, tutus and ballet skirts that have fallen out of the cupboard.

'Disguises?' asks Sid.

'No,' says Miss Diver. 'We used them in the staff pantomime. "Little Red Hiding Good." It was tremendous fun. Now, study these. They may give you a few ideas.'

She is not kidding! They are even worse than the other ones. And very high class, too. None of the blokes are wearing socks.

'If we could find out where these were taken we might be on to something – like that bloke, for instance. Cor!'

'It must be somewhere posh,' I say. 'All those suits of armour and that. Hey! What's that up there?'

'The same as what's up down there,' says Sid. 'The same

as what's up in every blooming photograph – acres of hampton!'

'I was referring to the flag,' I say. 'That's the frog job, isn't it?'

'You're right!' says Sid. 'This could be a valuable lead. We've narrowed the search down to France.'

'Mr Boris asked me to give you this and your survival kits.' A slim, groovy chick has come into the room and her cashmere cardigan brushes against my cheek as she hands Sid an envelope and each of us a small packet. I don't know what kind of perfume she is wearing but it is the sort that upper class birds always splash behind their lugholes and reminds me of freshly laundered knickers laid out on a shelf sprinkled with lavender. It goes with Hernia scarves and all that clobber.

I open my package and find two small Elastoplasts, a packet of Ovaltine Tablets and a tube of something called Xylocaine Gel. I can see myself surviving for about five minutes on this lot.

'What's this?' I say, waving the tube under the new bird's hooter.

'Oh that's wonderful,' she says. 'If you're in agony at any time – and let's face it, most of our agents are – rub some of this ointment on and you won't feel a thing.'

'Sounds great,' I say. 'Live now, pain later.'

'You've arrived just in time, Felicity,' says Miss Diver. 'As you know, L and N have just been recruited to the organisation. You can help me put them through their C Men Test.'

'You mean, ascertain their resistance quotient?' says the bird addressed as Felicity. 'How ripping? Where are we going to do it?'

'Look at this!' says Sid who has opened the envelope. 'Two plane tickets to Cannes. That's nice, isn't it?'

'No,' I say. 'Nice is about fifteen miles down the coast. They're quite different.'

'Shut up!' says Sid. 'You know what I mean. It's funny, isn't it? You noticing that flag and these tickets arriving. It could be more than a coincidence. I think Boris knows something and he's trying to tip us off.'

'You could be right,' I say. 'It's strange but I didn't take to him at first.'

'You're like that about everybody,' says Sid. 'Dead suspicious. There's something almost unhealthy about the way you find fault with everything – why are you taking your clothes off?' He is not talking to me but to the two birds who have got down to bra and panties while we have been nattering.

'We have to find out how liable you are to succumb to female blandishment, and take appropriate counter measures,' says Jenny Diver smoothing down the front of her coffee-coloured slip. 'We can't afford leaks with C Men.'

'We've lost some of our best agents because they allowed themselves to fall into the clutches of beautiful foreign spies who set out to enmesh them with their bodies. We have to find out if you can remain icy calm when exposed to provocation.' Felicity licks her lips. 'It's all jolly good fun really.'

'What were those counter measures you were talking about?' I say.

'Don't worry about those, darling,' purrs Felicity. 'We may not need to take any. I expect Mummy's boy's got oodles of yummy-wummy self control, hasn't he?' So saying the crude cow shoves her mit down the front of my trousers and helps herself to a handful of hampton.

'One-point-five seconds,' says Miss Diver looking from the outline of my erect prick to a stopwatch that has jumped into my hand. 'That's a record.'

'I wasn't ready,' I say. 'I didn't have time to turn my emotions off.'

'He's always been the same,' says Sid. 'No control. I'm afraid he's going to be a dead loss at this caper.'

Miss Diver glances from her stopwatch to the front of Sid's trousers. 'Take your hands away,' she says.

'But they'll fall down,' whines Sid.

'Take your hands away!'

Sid does as he is told, his trousers drop to the floor and his Mad Mick stands out proudly like the bow of a schooner.

'What do you know?' says Sid. 'It must be the central heating.'

Miss Diver shakes her head seriously. 'I don't know if we've got enough serum,' she says. 'These are the worst cases I've ever seen in the service.'

'Serum?' says Sid.

'It's an anti-sex drug that will render you free from temptation,' says Felicity. 'Once you've had the injection—'

'Injection?' I say.

'Only a little one,' says Miss Diver. She opens a drawer and produces a syringe like the one my Aunty Daisy uses on her roses.

'Have we got enough serum?' says Felicity.

Miss Diver disappears behind the desk and comes up with a smallish oil drum. She sloshes it about and it sounds almost full. 'Just enough,' she says.

I look at Sid and Sid looks at me. For both of us it is clearly a case of serum-scare 'em.

Miss Diver puts her can on the desk and sighs. 'It's a distasteful fact but the serum is applied most effectively directly after sexual intercourse. For that reason I must ask you to accompany me to the escritoire.'

'I don't feel like going,' says Sid.

But Miss Diver is clearly talking about the antique desk she has just climbed on to. Lying back against the tooled leather, she arches her back and slips off her knicks. 'Come,' she says. I can see that Sid is weakening – not in the hampton department, of course. That is still in what might be described as a state of rude health.

'This serum,' he says. 'It's not permanent, is it?'

'Not in every case,' says Miss Diver, parting a very shapely pair of legs and dangling them over the edge of the desk.

'Oh my gawd,' says Sid. Like a doomed man making his way to the scaffold, he stumbles towards Miss Diver who guides him between her legs and jerks forward like a trout snapping up a fly. There is a slapping noise which could be his bum-buffers making contact with Miss Diver's sit feature and the china mug holding half a dozen biros and a letter opener begins to rattle.

'This could be the last time!' groans Sid. 'Oh why did I ever allow myself to get into this?'

I don't attempt to answer this question because Felicity is playing the crumpet voluntary on my hampton and her technique is such that you have to pay it the respect of total attention. By the time that Sid has got the lids of the silver inkpots clicking like castanets, Felicity has finished her solo and is tucking my tingling tonk into her squidge box.

'Are you going to come quietly?' she purrs.

'It's very unlikely,' I gasp. 'Oooooooooooohhhhhh!!'

I never see either of these birds again so I don't have the chance to ask them about it, but I reckon that they must have been taught some special kind of muscle control. I can usually keep the cream of the British Empire in check until the time comes to send them in to No Man's Land but on this occasion there is an ugly rush for the saddle before I can get my bugle to my lips. Talk about the charge of the Light Brigade. The balls on the eve of Waterloo have nothing on my two when it comes to a mass exodus at the first sound of cannon fire. Sid tells me afterwards that it is exactly the same with him. It is over almost before it has begun.

'Right,' says Miss Diver, briskly swinging her legs off the desk – perhaps too briskly as far as Sid is concerned.

'I hope you were thinking of England, Felicity? Let's get down to business.' She plunges the syringe into the can and draws back the plunger with a loud slurping noise.

'Look,' says Sid. 'We don't have to go through with this, do we? We'll be good boys. I never liked girls much anyway.'

Miss Diver advances on Sid with her syringe at the on guard position. 'It's only a tiny prick,' she says.

'That's got nothing to do with it,' says Sid. 'It's sensitive just like any other prick.'

'I was referring to the injection itself,' says Miss Diver.

Sid seems unconvinced and backs towards the cupboard in which we disposed of the stiff. I am no hero when it comes to copping a shot of dick-deadener and I get behind Sid. I suppose that is part of the trouble. I step on his trouser leg, he stumbles back against me, I grab hold of him, and together we fall backwards into the cupboard. For a fraction of a second I catch a glimpse of Felicity's horror-struck face and the wicked glint of Miss Diver's syringe as she lunges at Sid's cluster. Then we are falling, falling, falling. A small square of light grows smaller and smaller and we plunge towards the next chapter.

## CHAPTER TEN

In which Timmy and Sid journey to Nice and are met by Desirée and her friend Gee Gee, a lady who introduces Timmy to the delights of the Eskimo Cocktail, the principal ingredients of which appear to be ice cubes presented in an unusual manner.

'Blimey!' says Dad 'It's disgusting. I never niffed nothing like it!'

'You want to get your hooter out and about a bit more often, don't you?' says Sid.

'That's enough from you, sponger,' says Dad. 'You ought to be ashamed of yourself coming round here in that condition. What's wrong with your posh house in Vauxhall? Why does our bath towel have to cop it?'

'Bath towel?' says Sid. 'That rag used to line the cat's basket when I was living here. Anyway, I didn't want to come round here. It was just the nearest place to where the sewer came out.'

It's terrible, isn't it? I thought at least we were falling into an underground river. It's the first time that I have ever wished I had the use of one of Dad's gas masks. How we got out constitutes a series of adventures too disturbing to relate in the sort of book bought mainly by clergymen's sons and the daughters of gentlefolk but I must say, I will never be able to look another Richard the Third in the faece again.

'That pong!' says Dad. 'I can't stand it.'

'Oh belt up!' says Sid. 'You should have got a snitchful before we cleaned up.'

I am dead worried because I have a date with Gretchen and I don't want her to start having doubts about my personal freshness programme. I have enough problems as it is, what with her minge being like a clenched fist and my hampton making less headway than a dumpling up a pea shooter.

'I don't know what you were doing down there, anyway,' sniffs Dad. 'You got a job with the Council, have you?'

Sid puts on his scornful look. 'I'm not in a position to diverge who we're under contract to but it's someone considerably higher than the Council I can assure you.'

Dad taps his hooter. 'Smells considerably higher and all,' he says.

'Supposing I said MI5 to you?' says Sid.

'I'd say you were round the twist. You're more like thirty-five if you're a day.'

'MI5, not am I five?!' I say. 'Oh Dad. If only I could tell you. This time I'm doing something of national importance. Just like you were when you were counting how many buildings were burning during the war. I'm off to Cannes tomorrow.'

'That's good,' says Dad. 'Working for Heinz, are you? Knock us off a crate of baked beans while you're there.'

It is funny, but once I get back to Scraggs Lane I find it difficult to believe that our experiences at the headquarters of Mission E actually took place. Am I really a C Man? Did I truly meet P and Boris and have it off with Felicity in the Debriefing Room? When Sid has gone, I sit on my bed and examine the only link with reality I have – no, not that – my airline ticket to Nice. When I look out of the window and see Mrs Dugdale combing her chinchillas it does not seem possible that a few hours ago I was plunged into the world of international espionage. Still, I suppose it must be like this for agents all over the world. You have to stop for a cup of cha and a wad sometimes. I take another look at the plane ticket and push it back into my genuine imitation leather wallet. I do wish it was a return.

My date with Gretchen is not a success and I have to take some of the blame on my own shoulders and other-parts. I have carefully nicked some of Mum's cold cream to ease things along and I reckon that it must have been a bit too cold. It was either that or the piercing North Easter streaking through all the holes the vandals have made in the shelter on the children's playground. Little bastards! They don't deserve all the money the council lavishes on them. The council ought to do something for the rest of us. All the couples who want to get their ends away and have nowhere to do it. We haven't all got cars, you know. The minute I get on the council there are going to be snogging cabins springing up all over Clapham and Wandsworth Commons like mushrooms. They will work on a meter basis and if you stay five minutes after a warning bell has gone, a built-in mechanism will tip you out of the side of the hut. You won't have to use the same sheets as anybody else because the bedding will advance like an automatic towel. It's a good idea, isn't it? I reckon that it will bring in so much bread that we will be able to halve the rates after six months.

This is all very well but it is not helping my relationship with Gretchen. The poor kid is in tears. Not just the pain but the frustration. She wants it just as much as me. If only I could get her to see a doctor. A local anaesthetic – there's no point in going a long way to have one – a little snip and – hey presto! Open season for furtling the furburger. I will have to get on to her about it when I get back – at this rate it's the only way I will get on to her.

When I meet Sid at the airport he is in a diabolical mood. There is an ugly swelling beside his right eye – no, as well as his nose – and it transpires that he and Rosie have had words. Apparently, he told her that he was taking an overnight bag to the South of France and she got the wrong idea.

'You haven't said anything about the outfit,' he says eventually. 'I suppose you don't like it either?'

'Well,' I say, trying to be tactful as always. 'I think the red, white and blue beret is going it a bit.'

'I knew you'd say that,' says Sid. 'And after all the trouble I went to painting it, as well. You've no idea how blooming difficult it is to stop the paint running on this felt.'

'I have,' I say. 'It's still running down the side of your nut – the bit that hasn't smudged, that is.'

'Blast!' says Sid. 'Anything else?'

'Well,' I say. 'The matelot's jersey with the hoops. That's Rosie's, isn't it?'

'How did you know?' says Sid.

'Because it's got a big saggy bit in the front where Rosie's knockers have been punching holes in it,' I say.

Sid looks really depressed. 'You must like the little moustache,' he says.

'What little moustache?' I say.

'Oh bugger!' says Sid. 'Don't say it's fallen off again! I don't know why I bother.'

'I don't know why you bother, either,' I say. 'And Sid. Do yourself a favour. Take that loaf of French bread out of the front of your bell bottoms. You'll get us both arrested.'

Sid whips out his loaf and yelps with pain – I think it must have been a crusty one. 'You're like your blooming sister,' he says. 'No imagination. Can't you see? I'm trying to act the part. If we're going to France we want to look like Frenchmen, don't we?'

'Why?' I say.

'It's obvious,' says Sid as if talking to a godfer (God

forbid: kid. Ed.). 'So we can blend into the background. So we don't raise suspicion. We're playing for high stakes, you know. You don't seem to be taking this assignment seriously. I bet you haven't got a French phrasebook, have you?' I shake my head and Sid smiles triumphantly. 'I have. I got it from the library. If this plane's got a postillion on it and he gets struck by lightning then I'm in business.'

But nobody on the plane gets struck by lightning. They don't get the chance to. The plane gets blown up before anybody can get on it. Yes! Amazing, isn't it?

'I expect somebody left a fag on,' says Sid. 'They're always telling you not to do it, aren't they?'

'Thank goodness we weren't on it,' I say.

'Exactly,' says Sid. 'You took the words right out of my mouth. We've had a lot of good luck today, haven't we?'

Sid is right. A number of strange things have nearly happened to us since we arrived at the airport. To start with there is the taxi that drives straight at us outside the terminus. I know the cabbies are a bit funny at Heathrow but there is no cause for that. Then there are the automatic doors. They only cut Sid's suitcase in half, don't they? And the escalators. The minute we get on them, they speed up and throw us down the luggage ramp. I nearly get on the plane before my hold-all. When flames come out of the hot-air hand dryer and the bloke on passport control tries to stab Sid, I begin to feel that this is not our day. It is not the best photograph that Sid has ever had taken but there is no need to react like that.

By the time we eventually board Air France Flight No. 1169 to Nice I am feeling quite edgy.

'We only need to get hijacked and that's it,' I say. 'It'll be Sea-Link for me every time. I'd vomit all the way to Boulogne rather than go through this lot again.'

Sid's scaly eyes are playing over the shapely limbs of the stewardess, a dark-haired beauty who looks as if she has had to borrow her kid sister's uniform. 'I wouldn't mind high-jacking her,' he says. 'High-jacking, low-jacking, you name it.'

'Come off it, Sid,' I say. 'You know what P said.'

'We haven't got there yet,' says Sid. 'It's all right on the journey. These Continental birds are all crazy for it you know. Watch this.' Sid tips his beret towards his hooter and whistles through his teds. 'Oy, darling,' he says, jerking his gunga din towards his rock and boulder. 'You seen Emanuelle, have you? How about making me a life member of The Mile High Club? Plenty good fucky-wucky, jig-jig, you savvy? And chuck in a bottle of after shave from the store cupboard while you're at it.'

The bird looks at Sid like he has crawled out of one of the thick paper bags. 'You are ze most disgusting man I 'av ever zeen,' she says. 'Take your 'and off my leg or I will pour scalding 'ot coffee over eet.'

'Stuck up bitch,' says Sid when she has gone. 'That's the Roman Catholic Church for you. They're all repressed. It was different during the war, you know. They couldn't do enough for you then. I knew this bloke who told me how far he got on a bar of chocolate. It wasn't even milk.'

'She doesn't seem to be too repressed down there,' I say. 'Look. She's sipping champagne out of that geezer's glass and his hand is running all over her like a Derby winner.'

'He won't get anywhere,' says Sid. 'She's a lesbian. I can spot them a mile off.'

'But she's put down her coffee pot – and – yes. They've both gone into the karsi.'

'There's probably a blockage. There was when I went in there.'

'Then why is the door quivering like that?'

'Because they've probably had to resort to violent measures to clear the blockage. Gordon Bennett! Do I have to explain everything to you? Have you no imagination?'

'I think they're having it off, Sid.'

'Having it off! A lesbian and a pouf?'

'How did you know he was a pouf, Sid?'

'They're all poufs, aren't they? All that drinking champagne and waving your hands about and smelling nice. What real man would descend to that in order to get his end away? I'd rather do without, myself. I'd rather preserve my manly identity. I turn my back on all this kinkiness.'

There is much more in this vein but, frustrated in my attempt to get a second cup of coffee, I drift off to sleep. Just as well really, because I miss the rocket attack on the aircraft. Everybody is talking about it when we eventually make an emergency landing at Nice – on the beach not the the airport. Honestly, you have never seen so much topless frippet running into the sea in your life. Like lemmings, they are – and lemons – and grapefruit – and some of them like blooming great melons. It must be a shock for them actually going in the briny after all those years of just looking at it and slapping suntan lotion over their knockers.

'I reckon we must have violated Liechtenstein air space,' says Sid.

'They don't have any air space in Liechtenstein,' I say. 'You have to lean over the border into Switzerland to breathe.'

Eventually, a coach arrives to take us to the airport and Sid unknots his handkerchief and rolls down his trouser legs. Honestly, he would be embarrassing even if he was not dressed like a mixture of Popov and Popeye.

'What we've got to do now is formulate a plan of campaign,' he says. 'We've been very fortunate in receiving this tip-off. Now we've got to make the most of it.'

'Right, Sid,' I say. 'But where do we start? We reckon the photographs were taken in a posh Mickey Mouse but there's millions of them round here – look at that bougainvillaea!'

'I missed her,' says Sid. 'I wasn't thinking of concentrating on the house. I was thinking we ought to find something that will lead us to the house.'

'A road?' I say. 'Surely that presents the same problem.'

'I'm going to present you with a handful of your own gnashers if you don't pull yourself together,' says Sid. 'I was talking about the distribution of the photographs. If they're flooding the country they've got to get into it. What better way than by post? If we hang around outside Cannes Post Office I reckon we'll see some geezer shoving a lorry-load of buff envelopes into the mail box. We follow him home and, hey voile! – or whatever they say out here. Which reminds me, I've left my phrase book on the plane. I wonder if the stewardess will get it for me.'

'She's still in the toilet with that pouf,' I say. 'I believe the firemen are having trouble getting them apart.'

'Blooming marvellous,' says Sid. 'I wondered why there was none of that stuff about "fasten your seat belts we are about to crash". The airline business is going to the dogs – and they don't give you those little boiled sweets any more, do they? You know, the ones that stop your ears falling off. What do you think of my plan, then?'

'It's got to be a mover,' I say. 'Provided that they are using the postal service and that they aren't posting the letters somewhere else.'

'Good,' says Sid. 'I'm glad it has your complete approval. As soon as we've checked through customs and I've had a Tom Tit, we'll start putting it into practice. I reckon we should be home in a couple of days.'

Nice airport is full of swankily dressed groovers kissing each other on the cheek and sporting tans that would get you asked to leave Smethwick Conservative Club and, once again, I can't help wishing that Sid was dishing out the couth a bit more. Even my lightweight lurex is getting a few doubtful glances so you can imagine how much the frogs reckon his clobber.

When he comes back from the karsi, he is looking double-choked. 'You've got to watch these bleeders,' he says, bitterly.

'What are you on about, Sid?'

'They've only nicked it, haven't they?'

'Nicked what, Sid?'

'The karsi. They must have only just put it in, too. You can see the footprints of the bloke that nicked it.'

'Sid!' I say. 'Really! I thought you knew about things like that. It's quite usual for the frogs not to have a pedestal and all that stuff. You squat down on those footprints and let yourself go.'

'Blimey!' says Sid. 'I don't fancy that. That's disgusting, that is! I'm not surprised none of the blokes wear turn-ups on their trousers.'

'You'll find that a lot of things are different over here,' I say. 'Now, what do you want to do? Have a nice cup of tea or get straight round to the Post Office?'

Sid puts on the expression he always wears when they play the National Anthem after the Epilogue. 'One thing I want to do is remind us both of the importance of this assignment. It was all right until we got here but now the fun and games have got to stop. You remember what P said?'

'No,' I say.

'Well don't forget it. I've noticed the way you've been clocking the birds around here. Any one of them could be a Russian spy. They know how to get it out of you.'

'Those two birds in London certainly did,' I say. 'OK Sid. I get the message. Be dead wary of any judy who tries to give me the old heave ho. Don't worry, I'll be on my mettle.'

No sooner have I squared my enormous shoulders and invested myself with a new sense of dynamism and purpose than a bird pushes her way towards us wearing a bikini that barely covers her raspberries – and I mean barely. She is not badly equipped in the pushing department either. 'Excuse me,' she says. 'It eez L and N, eez it not? I am sorree I am late meeting you. We do not zink zat you surv— I mean, the traffic eez very 'eavy thees time of the year.'

I turn to Sid expectantly. No doubt he will tell the lady to piss off, if not actually slap her round the mush a few times.

'Charming, I'm sure,' he says. 'Forever would be too short a time to wait for someone of your fragile and exquisite beauty. How do you fancy copping a few yards of stout British hampton up your velvet snatch?'

I cannot argue with the sentiments. These are beautifully expressed. But they seem slightly at odds with what Sid has just been warning me about.

'Ah hem,' I say. 'Sid—'

'Boris zent me,' says the bird. 'I am Desirée. 'E zink that you need car. Eet eez outside now.'

'That's great,' says Sid. 'Very considerate. He's a real gent that Boris. Can we give you a lift anywhere? My Marquis of Lorne is proceeding in a northerly direction at the moment.'

My initial feeling of relief when I hear Boris's name is tainted with wariness. There is still something about the man I do not trust. And all those things that have gone wrong since we left home. Were they really accidents?

'I am afraid zat you vill 'av to vait vor a vew minutes,' says Desirée. 'Ze car eez not quite ready for you. I am aving ze men give it a thorough overall.' She nods towards the exit doors and I see a couple of men bent over the engine of a Fiat. They seem to be fitting a metal canister connected to two wires.

'Some kind of petrol-saving device, is it?' says Sid.

'Oui,' says the bird. 'Vith zat in ze car you vill use very littel petrol. I, Desirée, guarantee it.'

'Well that's marvellous,' says Sid. 'Thanks a bunch, Daisy Ray. How's about a spot of in and out while we're waiting? I think I've just fallen deeply in love with you.'

Honestly, Sid makes the average Aussie sound like Little Lord Fauntleroy trying to grease his way to a new velvet suit. I expect Desirée to adjust her mit to the shape of Sid's cakehole but, to my amazement, she slips her arm through his and actually seems to reckon the idea.

'Zat vould be 'eaven chéri,' she pouts. 'Bring your so 'andsome ami and ve vill make ze promenade to ze beech. Zere ve can be alone. Ooh la, la, la, la!'

I am quickly beginning to realise that my fears regarding Desirée were groundless. Her back bumpers are pressed together so tight that you practically hear them squeaking when she walks and her brown, glistening body excites thoughts that some might consider unclean. Her mince pies are big and brown and there is a bright red carnation stuck behind her ear. When she smiles, her teds dazzle you, and her nostrils flare wider than Sid's bell bottoms. I wonder if she has a friend?

This question is soon answered when we come to a bar made of rush matting at the back of a sandy cove. Desirée gabbles something in French and the sandy cove shrugs his shoulders and pushes off. I am glad because I found his over-muscled body offensive.

'Close ze door and let us be alone,' says Desirée. 'Zis eez my friend, Gee Gee.' I suppose they call her that because of her teeth which are slightly protruding – amongst other things. I don't know if we have struck lucky but French birds seem to be particularly well-equipped in the knocker department.

'Pleased to meet you,' I say. 'My name's Tim – I mean, L.'

'Eet zoots you,' says the bird. 'Vot vould you like to drink?'

'I don't know,' I say. 'Something refreshing would be nice. It's a bit close, isn't it?'

'I hope so,' says Sid. 'Why don't you two push off behind that screen. Daisy Ray and I are very much in love and would like to be left alone.'

'Eez good idea,' says Desirée, feeling behind her for the catch of her bikini top. 'Gee Gee vill look after you. She always say she like big strong Engleesh boy.' So saying, she releases the catch on her bra and her boobs practically chase me from the room. Sid was obviously right about French birds. They are clearly desperate for it. Thank goodness help arrived just in time.

'And now, 'ot boy like cold drink.' Gee Gee gives me a look that would unseal an envelope at twenty paces and lifts the lid of an ice bucket. 'Vot eez your pleasure?' This bird is clearly not wearing anything underneath her ridiculously stretched T-shirt with 'McElrea was here' printed on it and I can see the dimples on her raspberries. What a good job I don't wear specs. They might steam up and I could stumble on top of her and do her a nasty injury with my erect doughnut driller. Thank God that another terrible accident has been averted.

'Well-er,' I say. 'I don't know, really. I'm not very good

on the old French drinks. An Oily Prat might slip down all right.'

'A Noilly Prat? With ice? Yes, I think you like lot of ice.' Gee Gee drops a couple of cubes into an empty glass and sashays towards me with a movement like something arranged by Frank Zappa. 'Take your jacket off. You eez 'ot.'

I put my arms behind me to start pulling off my jacket and the bird presses against my chest and ruckles her knockers up and down like she is rolling pastry. It is what might be described as a forward gesture and makes me feel that a kiss on the lips – or any other part of the body for that matter – might not be unappreciated. I lower my north and south and we engage cakeholes. Gee Gee's tongue shoots into my mouth faster than a mother-in-law streaking into a newlyweds' flat to make sure that it is good enough for her daughter, and her hand fumbles for my fly.

'I cool you down,' says the forward frog frippet. 'I give you eskimo cocktail.'

'That's nice,' I say, wondering what she is talking about. One thing that won't be a problem is a swizzle stick. Percy is stiffer than a giraffe's neck in a draught and you could stir a vat of toffee with him – though I would rather you didn't.

'Very nice.' To my surprise, Gee Gee raises the glass to her lips and takes the two ice cubes into her mouth. It is certainly a way of cutting down on your calories though I would not recommend it to get the party going.

My hampton has now broken cover and Gee Gee seizes it and shows me her tongue as she gives an electric shiver. Something about the way she looks into my eyes alerts me to what is about to happen and I suck in my breath. Gee Gee plucks open the buttons of my shirt and her cold, wet mouth begins to taxi southwards down my chest. 'You can't,' I say. 'No, no! You mustn't. It's – *Oh! Eeh! Ow! Ugh!* – quite nice really, isn't it?'

## CHAPTER ELEVEN

In which the trail leads to a mansion outside Cannes and Timmy finds himself under pressure from new friends, Suzanne and Marcia in unusual circumstances.

'That was a nice little interlude,' says Sid, 'we deserved that after our abstinence on the plane I'm glad I didn't succumb to the blandishments of that stewardess tart. What was Gee Gee like? You didn't say nay to her, did you? – get it? It's a play on words. You see, there's neigh what horses do and—'

'Yes, Sid,' I say hurriedly. 'Very funny. Actually, I'm feeling a bit numb. This bird only goes down on me with a mouthful of ice cubes, doesn't she?'

'Blimey,' says Sid. 'Sounds more like a snow job than a blow job. What was it like?'

'I don't know,' I say. 'I haven't felt anything yet. What was Desirée like?'

'Exquisite,' says Sid. 'She did things to me that were so disgusting I will treasure them for ever. Now, let's get this show on the road. Do you want to drive or shall I? I wish those birds had stopped long enough to show us how the controls work. They were round that corner like a dose of salts, weren't they?'

'And with their fingers in their ears too. Funny, that.'

Sid nods and switches on the ignition. There is a small flash and a 'phut' noise from underneath the instrument panel.

'Bloody marvellous,' says Sid. 'All that messing about and they still can't get it right. Just shows you what frog craftsmanship is like. I wish all those bleeders who buy foreign cars were with me now.'

We get the bonnet open eventually and Sid nods as if his suspicions have been confirmed. 'There's your trouble,' he says.

'What is?'

'No engine.'

'That's in the back.'

'Why didn't you say?'

'I thought you must have a special reason for wanting to get at the boot.'

Sid says something I last saw written in the gents at Finsbury Park Station and we expose the engine. 'We can get rid of this for a start,' says Sid viciously. 'Bloody petrol saver! We're only going to be here for a couple of days.' He rips out the canister and makes as if to throw it into one of the banks of flowers.

'Hang on!' I say. 'There's no need for that. It probably only needs a simple adjustment. Chuck it in the boot and we'll hand it back with the car. Somebody else can have the benefit of it.'

Sid goes on grumbling but he does as I say and we get back into the car. 'Hang on a minute,' I say. 'There's a note here. "Dear fiends" – they must mean friends – "if the—" there's a bit crossed out here. I can't read it. Looks like something, something, something explore.'

'Or explode,' says Sid. 'Except that that wouldn't make sense. It must be something about having a good time exploring. I wonder why they crossed it out? What does it say next?'

'It says "On the way to Cannes, do not use the brakes until you get to the Corniche".'

'What's the Corniche?' says Sid.

'Hang on a minute. There's a PS. "The Corniche is the

road that runs along the cliffs, full of dangerous hairpin bends and precipitous drops on to the rocks hundreds of feet below".'

'I see,' says Sid. 'They must have just changed the brake linings and wanted to give them time to settle.'

'Oh good,' I say. Sid does have his shortcomings but his mechanical knowledge can be invaluable on occasions.

A few minutes later we are bowling along a mountain road with a fantastic view of the sky-blue Mediterranean far below us. The wakes of speed boats criss cross each other like the vapour trails of jet planes and there isn't a cloud in the sky.

'This is the life!' says Sid. 'Wacko the froggies! Oh I do like to be beside the—'

'Do you think this is the way to Cannes Post Office?' I say. 'You must have to climb a long way to get your old age pension.'

'Don't worry about that,' says Sid. 'Lie back and enjoy it. We're starting to go down now. There's a sign there for "Chaussée Deformeé". Ever heard of it?'

'No, but they ought to do something about their roads. They're diabolical.'

'They're big on signs, the frogs, aren't they?' says Sid. 'Look at that one: "Danger! Virages 3km". I wonder what a virage is? Probably some kind of mirage. Fog, most likely. Well, we don't have to worry about that today.' He accelerates happily as we start to go down a steep incline.

'That's a funny sign,' I say. 'It looks like lots of Richard the Thirds raining down on you.'

'Most probably just what it is,' says Sid. 'Beware of blokes having a Tom Tit over the edge of the cliff. Dirty bastards, the French. I'm surprised they bother to warn you. Thank God we're not driving a convertible.'

He throws the jam (jamjar: car. Ed.) into the first bend

and we come out of it at about seventy. 'Blimey!' I say. 'You took that a bit fast didn't you?'

'You have to press hard to get anything out of these brakes,' says Sid, a bit grim-faced. 'Hang on!'

The next bend has a truck coming out of it and I think we go under it at right angles.

'Sid!' I scream. 'Are you mad?'

'The brakes don't work!' howls Sid.

'Are you pressing the right thing!?'

Panic-stricken, Sid jams his foot down and we start going even faster. 'Wh-e-e-e-e-o-o-o-o-wwwww!'

Sid swings the wheel to the right and I am forced to lean over the side of the car and clock a view of waves pounding rocks hundreds of feet below. 'S-i-i-i-id!!!!' I wrench at the hand brake and it comes away in my hand. This must be the end! Farewell to the dynamic duo. Even Denis Healey couldn't get out of this one. We are now heading down a straight bit at about a hundred and twenty towards a right angled bend with a precipice where the pavement ought to be. At the angle of the bend a gravel drive rises steeply, its entrance flanked by high wrought-iron gates.

'Hang on!' says Sid. What a bloody stupid thing to say! If I was hanging on any tighter I would be bending the seats in half.

Sid steers the jam straight for the drive and my nut jerks back as we take off as if hitting the up part of a switchback. There is a vicious screech of tyres biting into gravel and a blur of colour as we career past a jungle of exotic shrubs. The drive rises steeply and our speed begins to slacken. By the time a white stucco mansion hoves into view we are down to about forty and when we hit the Rolls parked outside, it is only with enough force to dent the number plate.

'Oh my gawd,' says Sid. He is paler than the winner of

the World Wanking Championships and we are both shaking like a couple of highly placed contenders. 'Let's get out of this thing!'

Sid does not need to say it twice. I never want to sit in a car again. We have just scrambled out and are taking a few deep breaths when there is the sound of frog voices approaching from the inside of the house. Of course, we could hang around and explain everything but without Sid's phrasebook there doesn't seem much point. Best to be retire behind a handy bit of trellis work and take a butcher's through the holes that have not been occupied by creepers. First through the door is an old bag wearing a bikini – or maybe it is a hundredweight of compressed prunes wearing a sling. Honestly, I don't like to be unkind but she should not do it. One look at her could put the mockers on your sex life for ever.

'Vite, vite!' she says. 'Ee eez wilting already. Ooh la la! Fi Fi, get ze splints!'

No sooner have I adjusted myself to this unpleasant sight than a geezer hoves into view. He is stark naked except for a mask and a french letter shaped like Donald Duck – I know, it takes me back a bit as well. Behind him come two knock out birds wearing the kind of underwear-pyjamas you would pretend not to look at if you were walking your old lady down Shaftesbury Avenue. Beside me I feel Sid stiffen – not in an unpleasant way, I hasten to add.

'Blimey!' he says. 'I think we've stumbled across it.' I examine the soles of both shoes before I see what he means. Another bloke has shown up carrying a camera, and a bird who must be Fi Fi is trying to perk up Donald Duck – or should it be Donald Dick? Either way, he is more Wilt than Walt Disney at the moment. 'This is their HQ!' hisses

Sid. 'This is where they take the photographs! Quick! we must inform P.' So saying, he turns on his heel, catches his foot in a creeper and dives into a conveniently placed swimming pool. Froggy warbles rent the air and I can hear Madam doing her nut as I drag Sid out and we scarper through the french windows and into the house. I don't have time to stop and value the stuff we sprint past but there is clearly a bit of money about. Up the marble staircase we go and Sid pauses as we dash round a corner.

'We'll have to split up,' he says. 'It's our only chance. Keep your pecker up, old bean, and if you get back to Blighty before me, give mater a real plonker from me.' I have never heard Sid talk like this before and I can only put it down to all those old war films they show on the telly. Like I say, he is very impressionable behind that stupid exterior.

'OK,' I say. 'Good luck.'

I don't stop to see where he goes but dash down the corridor and try the fourth door on the left – I was fourth in The West Clapham Wolf Cubs' egg and spoon race when I was a kid. The door opens and I find myself in a large bedroom with a verandah and built-in wall cupboards. I move towards the verandah but I can hear someone running by underneath so I duck back and open one of the cupboards. It is stuffed full of clothes – OK so I wasn't expecting banana skins. Shall I get inside it? I hear the sound of footsteps approaching down the corridor. I will get inside it. I press back into the deliciously ponging threads and slide the door to with my fingertips. No sooner has the darkness enveloped me than I hear a door opening and a long drawn-out female sigh. There is a pause and then the unmistakable sound of a zipper being unzipped – a zipper being zipped never has quite the same abandoned note about it. Another pause and the rustle of dress material. I hold my breath and wait – it is too cramped in the cupboard to hold anything else. Thirty seconds go by and I expel my breath. At the same instant, the door of the cupboard slides back and a hand presses a dress against my chest. I peer out to see one of the chicks who was at the session on the terrace. She is naked except for a tiny pair of scarlet panties and her enormous knockers heave like a couple of fenders hitched over the side of a vessel moored in a choppy sea. If she gives the game away I am lost. A mixture of panic and bravura grabs me.

'OK,' I say, advancing from the cupboard and jabbing one of my digits at her. 'This finger is loaded. Open your mouth and you get it straight between the eyes.'

Just the way I say it should terrify the bird out of her mind but she looks at me like I am collecting for a jumble sale. 'I'd rather open my legs and get it straight between the entrance to my you-know-what,' she say. 'Followed by something long, strong, and rhyming with sock. Marcia! Come and see what I've found.'

'You're English!' I gasp, taken aback by this strange turn of affairs.

'Of course I am,' says the bird. 'Leicester – and I wish we'd never left it.'

As she speaks, the adjoining door to the next room opens and the other half of the delectable duo on the terrace comes into the room. She is obviously naked beneath her housecoat, a fact better concealed when she draws the garment across the wide expanse of flesh revealed between pubes and boobs.

'What's up Suzanne?' she says. 'Ooooooh!'

'You're traitors!' I say. 'How could you betray your country in this shameful way? Those photographs are undermining the self control of the whole nation.'

'What is he on about?' says Marcia.

'Search me,' says Suzanne. 'I hoped he was some half-crazed rapist who was going to make brutal love to me while I made a show of putting up token resistance – amongst other things.'

'You know what I'm talking about!' I say. 'Those pictures of important people doing naughty things to each other.'

'You must be off your chump,' says Suzanne. 'We don't have any important people in *Countess Hardon's Handbook of Sexual Happiness*.'

'*Countess Hardon's Handbook of Sexual Happiness*?' I say.

Even as I repeat the words they begin to ring a bell. Now I come to think of it, I have seen the withered crone in the bikini somewhere before.

'Oh you must have had it,' says Marcia. 'Everybody in the country has. "How to achieve true sexual happiness with the aid of forty-four different vibrators, french letters shaped like garden gnomes and a range of ointments guaranteed to increase the sensitivity of your bank manager if no one else.'

'I know!' I say. 'It's a catalogue. It comes in a plain envelope so your mum won't find you with it. My mate tried one of those french letters and his bird ran out of the room screaming.'

'I know,' says Marcia. 'The only sensation they increase in me is one of disgust.'

It is dawning on me fast that Sid may have been guilty of jumping to the wrong conclusion. These birds clearly have less complicated thoughts in mind than the destruction of the British Emuire.

'You were talked into it, were you?' I say.

'Oh yes,' says Suzanne. 'Utterly. When we answered the advertisement we thought it was the kind of thing the

Sunday papers warn you about. You know, working as waitresses in a club and then finding that you have to sleep with the customers.'

'And being in the south of France we imagined that it would be just a step to Marseilles and the white slave trade,' chips in Marcia. 'We thought we'd end up in a brothel south of Suez servicing the unspeakable desires of hosts of over-developed camel dealers.'

'But it didn't work out like that?' I say.

'No,' says Suzanne. 'It was ever so disappointing. Nothing exciting has happened at all – except when one of the electric vibrators ran amok and destroyed a summer house.'

'But that man,' I say. 'The one with the thing on his thing on the terrace. Him and his mate. They must put it about a bit?'

Marcia shakes her head sadly. 'I think they keep it to themselves if they do anything with it. I tried to get Marcel going when we were doing the cover of *One Thousand And One Exciting Love Positions* and he got quite uppity. Said I was smudging his body make-up.'

Marcel is not the only one who is getting uppity. Down at crutch level percy is getting an attack of the instant rigids. This is becoming the kind of case he likes to work on. Suzanne gives me a look that strips me down to the Y-fronts and then rips them contemptuously aside.

'Who are you, anyway?' she says.

I take a deep breath. 'Would you believe that I'm a C Man?' I say.

Suzanne and Marcia exchange glances. 'They don't come round here very often,' says Marcia. 'What precisely are you working on?'

'I can't reveal too much,' I say. 'But it's to do with someone who's been taking pictures of orgies and—'

'Orgies! ?' interrupts Suzanne. 'Ooh! Now you're talking! You had a friend, didn't you?'

Marcia lets the housecoat drop from her shoulders and takes a step towards me. 'We haven't got time to wait for him,' she says. 'It's every girl for herself!'

'Talk dirty while you're doing it,' says Suzanne. 'I love that.'

'Ladies!' I say. 'Girls – please—!' My back hits the bed like it is attached to it by strong elastic and Suzanne launches herself on to my cakehole while Marcia rips my trousers down to ankle level. My Mad Mick rears into the air like the Lone Ranger and as Suzanne swamps me with knocker I feel two pairs of hands getting to grips with my growth sector.

'Ooh! Warm your hands on that,' squeals Marcia. 'That's the thermostat my system's been waiting for.'

'First served, first come – I hope,' pants Suzanne. She peels off her panties and nudging Marcia aside, scrambles astride my unprotesting body. 'Now you see it, now you don't,' she says. 'Ooh, that's heaven. I'd forgotten what it was like.' She starts to bounce up and down and that old jungle rhythm starts throbbing through my loins. It is in situations like this that I always wish I had more parts. There are so many things you could be doing to birds, aren't there? So many places to touch, so many places to— I read the look of desperate need in Marcia's eyes and my heart melts – only my heart you will be glad to hear.

'Ding, ding!' I say. 'Room for one more on top.'

After that things got a bit confused and there are moments when I feel like a bootlace in a can of worms. I keep scratching my leg and finding that it belongs to someone else. One thing about working for Countess Hardon, it clearly keeps you up to date with tricky dicky positions. It also helps if you are double-jointed. I am not when we start but at the end of our session I am not so sure.

The late afternoon sun is slanting past the open shutters when I eventually lie back without either of the birds on top or underneath me. It has been a good afternoon's work by any standards and I think that P would be pleased with me. Sid, too. I wonder where he is? Ah well, I will have a little snooze and find him later. Marcia and Suzanne – nice girls – are asleep on either side of me and I close my mince pies and prepare to join them.

But I do not join them. Hardly have I become vaguely aware of a sound like that of a doorknob being turned stealthily than something hard is jammed against the side of my temple. I open my eyes and see a sight that strikes terror into my jam tart.

## CHAPTER TWELVE

In which the plot takes a thrilling turn.

Standing by the bed is a familiar, squat figure wearing a smock and holding an automatic vibrator. Its ugly pink nozzle quivers inches from my head. The intruder's features are unrecognisable behind a tightly stretched french letter on which is stamped: 'Export Division. Ghana. Medium Size'.

'Don't move!' says the stranger in an understandably muffled murmur. 'This battery operated Pleasure-Probe is turned up to twice the number of revs the hardiest nymphomaniac is capable of withstanding. One false move and I'll bore a hole in your nutsky!'

'You don't fool me, Boris!' I say. 'I suspected it was you all along. Take off that french letter and come quietly.'

'You're in no position to make ultimatums!' snarls Boris. 'Get off that bedsky!'

'What's happening?!' squeals a terrified Suzanne. 'Who are you?'

'Silence!' snaps Boris. 'One more word and you will share the fate of this foolish young man. You! On your feet!' He jabs the vibrator towards my goolies and I scramble over Marcia like she is the last fence in the Grand National and I have half a length over the rest of the field – in fact I don't have half a length over anybody at the moment. Percy does not like the vibrator and is settling down on his two travelling companions like he is trying to hatch them. 'Right,' says Boris. 'Now we will go outside and I will – UH!' He slumps to the floor as Sid bashes him over the nut with a combined Japanese rubber woman and pyjama case.

'Well done, Sid!' I say. 'Thank God you came!'

'Doesn't look as if I was the only one,' says Sid, taking a quick butcher's at the cowering birds. 'Come on, let's get out of here!'

He doesn't have to say it twice and I leap over the stirring Boris and race him down the marble corridor. Countess Hardon appears, shrieking, at the top of the staircase but we push past her and flow down the steps to the hallway. That photograph in the catalogue must have been taken about twenty years ago. Now, she is so wrinkled that she looks like the flesh round an elephant's arsehole. We rush out on to the terrace and down the steps to the summit of the circular drive. Our car is still boxed in by the Rolls. Behind us can be heard a muffled roar of rage and female screams.

'Get in!' shouts Sid. 'Not that one—! The Rolls!' We leap inside and Sid releases the hand brake. Slowly, the car starts to roll down the incline. I look behind us and, as we pick up speed, Boris can be seen leaping into our car.

'He's after us!' I shriek. 'Faster, Sid. Faster!'

'I can't go any faster, you berk!' says Sid. 'There was no key in the ignition. We're taxiing!'

'He'll catch us up in seconds!' I say. 'What are we going to do?'

'We'll have to try and fool him,' says Sid. 'First bend we come to, we both dive out and let the car go over the cliff. With a bit of luck, he'll think we were in it.'

It is at moments like this that you realise that Sid is sheer magic. What a great idea. I don't have time to tell him because we shoot out of the gates and nearly go over the cliff. I will swear that we have two wheels over the edge.

Somehow, we get round the bend and another sharp turn looms up fifty yards ahead.

'Come on!' says Sid. 'This is it!' He jams his foot on the brake and opens the door. I look in the driving mirror and see Boris coming up fast behind us.

'It's no good!' I say. 'He'll see us!' But Sid isn't there any more. I am alone in a Rolls Royce heading straight for a two hundred foot drop. For a moment I freeze. And then I realise how much I mean to myself. As the car sends up a cloud of dust at the brink of the precipice, I press open the door and throw myself sideways. The impact knocks all the wind out of me and when I stop rolling, one of my legs is dangling in space. I pull myself to safety and look up. The Fiat is hurtling towards me. Behind the french letter I see Boris's features contract as he stamps on the brake pedal – and again, even harder.

Then he is gone. Past me and into space. Curving out in a wide arc, following the Rolls on to the wave-covered rocks below. There is a 'crump!' and half a second later a blinding explosion that throws pieces of metal – and possibly, Boris – high into the air. They spin lazily and then drop back into the now quiet water. Only a couple of cushions mark the spot where the cars have disappeared.

# CHAPTER THIRTEEN

In which surprise follows surprise and all – and more – is revealed.

Three weeks later we are back in England. It takes us all that time to hitch hike across France. My plates of meat are disaster areas by the time we get on the ferry at Calais – and embarking is no picnic, I don't mind telling you. Have you ever hung upside down under an articulated lorry for twenty minutes? I can't recommend it. Frankly, I think our progress across France would have been a lot quicker if Sid had not insisted on waving a small Union Jack at every vehicle that came near us. Most of them accelerated and quite a few slowed down just long enough to shout the kind of things frogs write on lavatory walls – only, of course, most of their toilets don't have any walls which is probably why they have to shout things like that to get them out of their systems – or cisterns, more like.

It is all so blooming ridiculous because, of course, Sid and I are national heroes. We only have to get back to P and tell him about Boris and we will probably be knighted. Mum will be so chuffed and it will be nice to think that we have saved Britain. If you only do it once in your life it means something, doesn't it? The only black spot on the horizon is the thought of Dad coming to the Palace. I hope he waits outside the railings. I must have a discreet word with the Court Chamberlain about it.

The picture of Dad chatting up Her Maj with the tails of his morning suit tucked inside his long woollen coms is just one of the things that is agitating my mind as we eventually stumble into the vestibule that conceals the entrance to Mission E. There is still an 'out of order' sign on one of the lifts – but not the same one as before.

'Cunning,' says Sid, who has been getting even more balloon-bonced since he saw off Boris. 'Very cunning.'

'What are you on about, Sid?' I say.

'Don't you see?' says Sid, allowing a complacent smile the freedom of his chops. 'It's a double double bluff. This time the lift we want *is* the one with the 'out of order' sign on it.'

'Sid,' I say. 'Don't you think—'

But it is too late. Sid has flung open the door and disappeared with a wild shriek. 'Stupid, bloody fools!' he says when I have hauled him out. 'Look! I've lost the pom pom off my beret. All through France and I have to lose my pom pom on my own doorstep.'

'Tough,' I say. 'Still, you're not as oily as you were last time.'

But Sid refuses to be comforted and his mood does not improve when we get into one of the lifts and start trying to find the secret button that will open the sliding panel. We press every button in the lift fifteen times and all we do is stop at every floor in the building fifteen times. The caretaker is very narked about it. 'Why don't you go and play in the park?' he says. 'Couple of grown men behaving like kids. Get out of it before I call the police!'

'Have a care my good man,' says Sid. 'We are engaged upon work of national importance and failure to co-operate in our endeavours could earn you a bunch of fives up the bracket!'

The bloke is unimpressed by Sid's muscle power and has actually pushed off to call the fuzz when we find that you have to push the basement button twice to open the secret door – we might have guessed that it had something to do with the basement button earlier because there isn't a basement.

'At last!' says Sid as the panel closes behind us and we head towards the lift. 'I was getting so frustrated out there. So near and yet so far. Know what I mean?'

'Definitely, Sid.' It is like my relationship with Gretchen. I wonder how she is? Pining for me no doubt. I have an idea which might solve our problems and as soon as P has fixed up a date for the ceremony at Buckingham Palace I will nip round and try and put it into practice.

The lift doors slide open and we tumble out into the corridor.

'Here we are,' says Sid. 'Now, which office was it?'

'I don't know,' I say. 'Maybe it was this one.' I open the door six inches and peer round it. A group of keen-looking young blokes are clustered round a more senior cove who is clearly their instructor. 'Right, gentlemen,' he says. 'Today it's unarmed combat and I'm going to show you the most deadly and undetectable weapon you can use – the icicle. Used as a dagger it can effectively silence an adversary, yet have disappeared completely within minutes of the deed having been done – leaving, of course no incriminating evidence.' An awed murmur runs round the gathered throng. The instructor looks pleased with the impression his words have made. 'Right, to practise,' he says. 'Carruthers, come up here.' I crane forward and see that the instructor has a dish in front of him on which is laid a long, dagger-like icicle. 'Ready Carruthers?'

Carruthers is obviously dead keen and he brushes the hair from his eyes and nods urgently. It is clear that I have stumbled across a training session of Britain's Secret Service elite. 'Snatch up your test icicle – *No, Carruthers*! I said your *test icicle*!'

'What's happened?' says Sid.

'A bloke's just ruptured himself,' I say, closing the door. 'It's tough, this business.'

'You don't have to tell me that,' says Sid. 'Come on, I think it's this one.' He flings open the next door and we find ourselves in Miss Diver's office. She is not there but I recognise it by the photograph of Screaming Lord Sutch on her desk. 'Here we go,' says Sid. 'I hope you-know-who is careful to use the flat edge of her sword.' He gives a sharp rat-tat-tat on P's door and throws it open without waiting for a reply. P's hands are below the desk in furtive fashion and the expression on his face changes from one of anger to stupefied amazement when he recognises us. 'You—!' he gasps.

'That's right, Squire,' says Sid. 'Bit of a surprise, eh?'

P's mouth hangs open and he seems to be fighting to find breath. His hands appear above desk level and I see that they are covered with white sticky stuff. Oh dear, I hope we haven't barged in at an awkward— wait a minute! What is that at his finger tips! ? Not – no, it can't be! – but it is! Harold Wilson! Our glorious leader's mug is fastened to his sticky digits. Only in the form of a tiny cut-out photograph of course but it is enough to set the mind racing. What is he doing and why are all those other photographs spread across his desk?

'You swine!' says Sid. 'So you're in on it too!'

P springs to his feet and a folio of filthy photos and a tin of Cow Gum falls to the floor – for sticking to cows there is nothing better. 'Yes!' He snarls, a maniacal gleam coming into his eyes. 'But you'll never get me!' So saying, he makes a dash for his private bathroom.

'Stop him!' shouts Sid. I make a desperate dive but I am not fast enough. P leaps on to the lip of the lav, pauses wild-eyed for a moment, and jumps, pulling the chain as he goes. There is a familiar gurgle from the cistern and he is gone.

'Blast!' says Sid. 'We've lost him.'

'He won't get away,' says a familiar voice behind us. 'I'll throw a cordon round every sewerage works in the Greater London area. He won't slip through the net.'

'He'll slip through anything, if our experience is anything to go by,' says Sid. 'Wait a minute— It's you!'

We both stare at the newcomer and our mouths drop open wider than a tart's legs when the Nigerian Fleet is in port on a good willy visit.

'That's right,' says Boris. 'It's me. Welcome home boys.'

'But you're dead,' I say. 'At least, I hope you are. I mean—' I start to edge behind Sid who is trying to edge behind me.

'Don't worry,' says Boris. 'You have nothing to be afraid of. I am good guy. Ask anyone at the Krem – I mean MI6. I have had my suspicions about P for months now. Ingenious, wasn't it? What perfect cover for a man intent on taking over Britain – head of her most secret espionage echelon.'

Sid wipes Boris's spit off the front of his matelot T-shirt. You try saying espionage echelon. 'Is that what he was going to do?' he asks.

Boris nods. 'Yes. He planned to step into the vacuum caused when the whole population were fornicating in the streets.'

'I'm sorry,' I say. 'You'll have to take me back to the beginning. Why did P hire us if it was him who was behind everything?'

'Because he had to,' says Boris. 'If he hadn't taken action then people would have wondered why. Anyhow he was determined to liquidate you before you discovered anything.'

'So it wasn't you who tried to kill us in Nice?' says Sid.

'No, it was one of P's agents dressed up to look like me. He was suspicious that I was suspicious and he wanted to put the blame on me.'

'Blimey,' says Sid. 'It's complicated, isn't it? So P sent us to Nice?'

'No,' says Boris. 'I did. But I let P think that you were on to something so that he would show his hand.'

'You mean, by killing us?' I say, thinking of all the ways we nearly bought it on the way to France.

Boris looks uncomfortable. 'That's not a very nice word,' he says. 'Anyway, the department would have paid for the funeral.'

'That is fair,' says Sid. 'You've got to admit that's fair Timmo.'

'Oh shut up!' I say. I am getting a bit choked with the espionage business. 'What I don't understand is how you would ever have pinned it on him, if we'd have snuffed it and not come back to catch him at it.'

'Simple,' says Boris. 'Four weeks ago, I had a highly sensitive recording device built in P's watch – without him knowing of course. Every move he made against you was recorded and could have been used as evidence that would destroyed him. Had you died, your sacrifice would not have been in vain.'

'That's nice,' says Sid.

'Is this the watch?' I say. 'The date watch that appears to have stopped at the beginning of last month? Mickey Mouse's nose has fallen off and got wedged under the hour hand.'

'Fucksky!' explodes Boris. 'Heads will roll over this when I report back to the Politburo.'

'Ah well,' says Sid. 'No harm was done, was it? You know, it's a bit funny, but for a moment my mate and I thought that you might be a Russian agent. Stupid, isn't it?'

'It's that USSR on your smock,' I say.

'USSR?' says Boris. 'Oh that. That's – er United Services Squash Rackets. What could be more British than that?'

'What indeed,' says Sid. 'It just goes to show how easy it is to get a silly idea in your head, doesn't it?' He leans forward confidentially. 'I suppose we'll get a medal, knighthood, something like that?'

Boris shakes his head. 'Regretfully, the work of Mission E is so secret that we can make no award that would draw attention to its existence.'

'Oh dear,' says Sid. 'You couldn't leave a couple of CBEs on the edge of the desk and look the other way? We wouldn't say where we got them.'

'Definitely,' I say.

Boris shrugs. 'As the new head of Mission E, I wish I could do something for you. But it is impossible. Your reward will have to be that of knowing what you have done for Mother Russ – I mean, the old cunt – I mean the old country.'

'Very well, Squire,' says Sid. 'If that's the way it's got to be, so be it. Back to Clapham and Mum's the word. At least we know that we leave the country in good hands.' We move to the door and Sid pauses with his hand on the handle. 'There's only one thing about this lot that puzzles me,' he says. 'In the books there's always a beautiful bird mixed up in the din-dem-denni – the bit at the end. We don't seem to have that.'

A strange expression settles on Boris's unlovely face and he grips the bottom of his smock purposefully. 'Not so fast, cheeky!' he says. 'You haven't seen anything yet.' The smock whips up like a venetian blind being released and two enormous knockers are revealed.

'Cripes!' says Sid. 'It's a woman!'

'You betsky!' says the bird making a dive for Sid. 'Come here comrade! I have need of your services. All work and no Jack make Borisova a dull girlsky!'

The last I see of Sid he is pinned down with one of Boris's knockers on either side of his head. I think he is trying to say something but the words are understandably somewhat muffled and snatched away when the lift doors close in front of my face.

## CHAPTER FOURTEEN

In which Timmy attempts to achieve a happy ending with Gretchen.

We tell Rosie that Sid has been run over by a truck. Frankly, when we see him at the Bolingbroke Hospital it is difficult to tell the difference.

'I never want to go through anything like that again,' he says when Rosie nips out to change his library book. 'She was like a wild animal. I thought she was going to kill me.'

'She was responding to *your* animal magnetism,' I say. 'It just shows how careful you've got to be. Your power over women is a two-edged sword.'

'My sword doesn't have any edges on it at the moment,' groans Sid. 'Rosie keeps dropping little hints about how nice it's going to be when I get home but I don't think I'm going to be up to it.'

'You will in a few days,' I comfort him. 'Keep sipping the broth and you'll be up to it like a swallow to its nest.'

In many ways, Sid's little accident is a good thing because it stops Rosie asking where he has been for three weeks. Also he needs the rest, poor old sod. I ask Sister Duff how he is making out and she says that apart from the time when Teddy Savalas came up on the telly and he dived out of bed, he is making good progress.

I leave Sid, having eaten all his grapes – well, he was having difficulty finding the strength to spit out the pips –

and make contact with Gretchen. To my relief, she is dead chuffed to hear from me and quite impressed when I tell her that I had to go abroad on a case. Best of all, she says that the bird she shares a room with has gone back to Exeter for the weekend and that she is all on her tod – nudge, nudge, wink, wink. What could be better? If I can't crack 'The Case Of The Padlocked Fanny' now, then I never will. Especially as I have a plan.

It came to me when I found the remains of my Survival Kit in one of my pockets. I had eaten all the Ovaltine Tablets – and one of the Elastoplasts – but the tube of Xylocaine Gel was as intact as Gretchen's fun feature. It occurs to me that this gel stuff is in fact a local anaesthetic and that if we apply it to the affectionate area then percy can make a grand entrance without causing any discomfort. Good thinking, eh? You can see how my time in the Secret Service has paid dividends. At last I will be a C Man who has come into his own.

Of course I don't go straight round to Gretchen's place and start unscrewing my tube. I am too sophisticated for that. I know that a woman has to be brought to the boil gently. If you turn the heat up too high too fast, you spoil them. So what do I do? I pamper her, don't I? Buy her a swift half, then round to Monty's Whelk Stall for a plate of peeled prawns – pity it comes on to rain, but you can't have everything – *then* back to her place. That way she has been treated like Royalty and is prepared to do anything for you. It may cost a few bob but, believe me, it's worth it in the long run. When we go up the stairs to her flat I really feel that this is going to be my lucky evening – it needs to be because I haven't been home yet and I know the kind of reception that Dad is going to give me. I have kept the gel in my trouser pocket so that it is nice and warm – considerate again, you see? I hate to keep drawing attention to it but you have to learn these things – and by the time I get the top off it is practically liquid. The minute we get inside the flat, Gretchen starts peeling off her threads and it is obvious that the briefing I gave her during our meal at Monty's has worked her up to fever pitch.

'Oh! I want so much, so much!' she moans, rubbing her hands across her belly. She lies back naked on the bed and turns her beautiful soft, brown eyes on me and – cor!!

I am almost crying with frustration as I sit on the bed and wrench my knickers off. At last, I am ready and, though I say it myself, I have never seen percy in better condition. If the Spaniards nicked the Rock of Gibraltar I could produce a superior substitute immediately. I grab the gel and after a few kisses which practically rearrange our features, I start preparing the ground – or the mound, more like. Gretchen is not slow to lend assistance and in no time we have used most of the tube.

'Do you feel anything?' I say.

'I don't know,' says Gretchen. 'Let us try.'

Here we go. The moment of truth. I am sweating as I rise to my knees and station myself between Gretchen's shapely thighs. I position percy at the portal and look into Gretchen's eyes. She bites her lip and nods. I breathe in and drive percy forward. There is the customary resistance and then – Gretchen has closed her eyes but they suddenly open and a smile spreads across her face like the sun coming up. Her hands which have been tightly squeezing my arms release their grip.

'Oh yes!' she breathes. 'Yes!'

I try and smile but a horrible fear has seized me. I can't feel anything. The bloody Xylocaine Gel is working on me! Gretchen's face clouds over and together we look down towards my crutch. Totally desensitised, percy wilts and droops like a snowdrop pinched by an early frost. I think I might burst into tears. It hardly seems fair, does it? After all I have been through as a private dick, I have arrived at a dead end.